BELLA'S TOUCH

A MORGAN'S RUN ROMANCE

M. LEE PRESCOTT

Bella's Touch

By

M. Lee Prescott

Published by Mt. Hope Press
Copyright 2022, M. Lee Prescott

Published by Mt. Hope Press
Copyright 2022, M. Lee Prescott ISBN: 978-1-7379034-6-8 (print)

Cover Design by Ashley Lopez
Image: iStock.com/simonapilolla

http://www.mleeprescott.com/

To my sisters with love.

CHAPTER 1

"Hey, aren't you working today?" Tom Jacobi asked, observing his sister in jeans and a work shirt pulling on her riding boots.

The remains of her breakfast on the table, Bella looked up, smiling as she reached for her coffee mug. "Morning. I have the night shift tonight, so I'm not going in till noon. I thought I'd take a ride this morning."

"Alone?"

She rolled her eyes, brushing a strand of dark brown hair from her cheek. "I've gone a bunch of times with you. I know the trail."

"No one's riding alone right now with the mountain lion sightings. Ranch rules. Guy was attacked last week."

"Okay, then I'll ride around the ranch, then take some laps on one of the tracks."

"Not today you won't. We've got time trials this morning, which is why I can't go with you." Tom lived and worked at Valley Stables, a vast property north of the town of Saguaro Valley. The dream of two wealthy friends, the ranch trained and raced prize thoroughbreds and also ran a small wild horses rescue program. Tom was the assistant manager of both operations, and as such, lived in a beautiful farmhouse halfway between the thoroughbred stables and the barn that housed the wild horses and stable horses, several corrals and round pens behind it.

Hands on hips, Bella said, "Tommy, look at me. I'm ready to go. I only want to go out for an hour or so. Couldn't one of the guys go with me?"

"Not the stable crew, but I suppose I could spare someone at the barn. Grace is coming to work with Dusty in a bit, so she'll be around." Tom's fiancée, Grace McGraw, lived in town, but spent many days and some nights at the ranch. Even though Grace worked at her father's hardware store in town, she had bonded with one of the wild horses, a Kiger whom she had named Dusty. Thus, she spent most of her free time with Dusty and Tom. "And after your joy ride, you can give us an hour's work to make up for pulling one of my guys from his work."

"Deal!"

"I'll call Whip." Tom grabbed his phone and stepped out on the back deck, the western mountains stretched out in front of him. He returned shortly. "If you get down there pronto, Whip says he'll go with you. He's saddling two horses right now."

"Thanks, big brother," she said, caramel eyes sparkling as she gave him a hug.

Tom grinned. "Get out of here, and be careful."

Bella had moved from Montana to the Valley two months earlier and was living at the farmhouse with her brother. According to her, the arrangement was temporary, only until she got settled and found a place. Tom insisted that she could stay forever and secretly hoped she would. Bella was good company and a great cook. Then he and Grace announced their engagement and things changed. Bella told him she would begin immediately to look at condos in town and on the river. A wedding date had yet to be determined, and as far as Tom could tell, Bella had yet to go condo shopping.

A warm breeze blew through the yard as Bella headed down the hill. As she neared the beautiful newly built barn, she removed her work shirt and tied it around her waist. It was going to be a hot one. Gentle nickering and the scuffling of hooves sounded as she stepped into the cool, dark space, the smell of fresh hay all around her. She could see two horses saddled and tethered to a fence post just outside the door at the opposite end. Several men were leading other horses out to the fields and corrals, and she said hello as she passed by.

Greg Patterson emerged from one of the stalls leading a sturdy dun-colored horse. Like most of the wranglers, Greg was strong and lean, his curly dark hair stuffed under a worn Stetson. A real charmer, his brown eyes and good looks had caused many a Valley woman to swoon. So far, he remained unattached.

"Morning, Greg, morning, Dusty," Bella said as she came to pet the horse's broad, soft nose. Such a gesture would have been unthinkable two months ago for anyone but Grace.

"Hey, Bella. Whip's got your rides all set. He had to run up to the stables, but said he'd be back in five."

"Thanks. Can I help you with anything while I wait?"

"I think we're set, thanks. Only one still in the barn is Ghost, and it takes two of us to drag his sorry ass out."

Bella nodded and peeked into the last stall, separated by an empty space at the far end of the barn. The magnificent white stallion snorted and pawed as she passed by. One of five wild horses to come to Valley Stables several months ago, Ghost was the last to be gentled. Between Tom and Nick Parker, a horse whisperer who worked at Morgan's Run, they had managed to get a rope on him, and occasionally a blanket, but that was it. He still needed to be in a separate corral from the other horses, and he viewed Dusty, in particular, as his biggest rival.

"Don't go near him unless you want to get nipped. He's nasty," a voice said from behind her.

She turned to find Whip Kittredge, her brother's unofficial right-hand man, leaning against a stall door. "He's sure gorgeous." Bella smiled at the wrangler. *And so are you.* She followed the tall, laconic cowboy with shoulder-length blond hair, beard, and mustache, as he strolled toward her. Some people called Whip "Wild Bill Hickok," but Bella had seen photos of Bill Hickok, and the showman and folk hero had nothing on this guy. His smoky-gray eyes shimmered with warmth as he neared, craggy features aligned and perfect when he smiled. *Wild and woolly, but oh so sexy!*

"You ready?"

"Sure am." As he passed by, she realized too late that she'd been gawking. Whip stood beside Galahad, a stable horse from up the hill. A retired racehorse, Galahad had been bought for stud. Beside them, Whip's Appaloosa, Calico, waited patiently. "You brought Galahad down?"

"Yup. Boss's orders. He's a gentle ole guy."

"Yes, he is," Bella said, coming to scratch and pet the black thoroughbred who nickered and nudged her affectionately. "Galahad and I are old friends. But how'd you get him down here so quick?"

Whip smiled. "I delegated. One of the crew up there brought him down. They move fast."

"I guess so." She easily mounted the steady horse, settling herself in the saddle. As Whip adjusted her stirrups, she noticed the shotgun strapped to Calico's saddle. *Cougar defense*, she thought and suddenly felt guilty interrupting his work to babysit her. Mountain lion sightings were almost a daily occurrence now, which made her little joy ride a risk. "Thanks for doing this, Whip. I hope it's not going to make everyone's day tougher."

"Not at all. The guys'll just work faster and harder."

"That's what I mean! My brother says I owe you an hour's work when we get back."

"Lucky us," he said, effortlessly mounting his enormous black-and-white-spotted horse in one fluid motion. "Come on, buddy," he said, making sounds somewhere between a click and a kiss.

CHAPTER 2

In most places, the trail was wide enough for the two horses to be side by side. As they proceeded at a languid pace, they conversed about the weather, the ranch, and other innocuous subjects, each keenly aware of the other's nearness. From the moment his boss's sister had arrived, Whip had been smitten by the dark-haired beauty, with her soft caramel eyes and her intoxicating scent of bergamot and desert rose. Out of his league, he knew, but a guy could dream. When Maggie Morgan had gone into labor next to the corral several months earlier, he had marveled at Bella's gentleness and expertise as a midwife as she cared for the terrified woman. Bella was a healer, something sacred in his opinion.

Despite her dismissal of her riding prowess, Bella was an experienced horsewoman, comfortable and confident in the saddle. Galahad sensed her confidence and trotted along, unfazed as she shifted in the saddle and threw her head back in laughter. She had a deep, very sexy laugh.

As they rode, his eyes constantly scanned their surroundings. "You're looking for the cougars, aren't you?" she asked.

He grinned. "Cougars, javelinas, rattlesnakes, scorpions, you name it. Doesn't pay to relax your vigilance anywhere out here."

"Have you seen one? A lion, I mean?"

"Not here, but plenty back home."

"Which is?"

"Vancouver Island."

"British Columbia? You're Canadian, then?"

"Dual citizenship."

"Wow, I wouldn't have figured that," she said, gazing at him in surprise.

He shrugged. "Most everyone here is from somewhere else. Look at you and your brother."

"I guess."

A rustle in the nearby brush caught his attention, and Whip reined in Calico, reaching over for Galahad's bridle. "Whoa, boy."

As they watched, a group of six javelinas emerged from the brush and crossed the path. Since horses and riders were downwind, the poor-sighted creatures appeared to be unaware of their presence. Neither Galahad nor Calico made a sound. When the pig-sized peccaries disappeared, they continued.

"They are the funniest creatures, aren't they?" she said.

"Look like wild boars, act like wild boars, and don't much like people. They're also a favorite food of the mountain lion."

"Really?"

"Them and horses."

"Did you have javelina where you grew up?"

"Nope. Javelina like the heat."

They rode about ten minutes more before Whip turned toward a stream bordering the trail. "Let's stop and give 'em a drink,, then we'd better turn back," he said, slipping off Calico and letting the horse go to the water. He then came to help her down, his hands grasping her waist as she slid off.

Bella felt her face heat up and knew she was blushing. "Thanks," she said, stepping back.

He grinned. "No problem."

"So, Vancouver Island...that must've been a cool place to grow up."

He shrugged. "Probably not all that different from where you guys were. Montana's pretty spectacular."

Bella sat on a fallen log near him. "I've never been to Vancouver. What's it like?"

"Where we are, wild. My dad was a logger, but when the mill closed down, he opened an adventure tours company. It's pretty successful, actually. He wanted me to stay and work for him, but schlepping a bunch of touristas around isn't my idea of fun. I love horses. I knew I wanted to work on a ranch."

"So, your parents still live there?"

He nodded. "My parents and my sister. She works with Dad. My mom's a blogger, 'Gold River Belle.' I hear she's popular, but I don't follow her."

"What about other brothers and sisters?"

He stood abruptly. "You sure ask a lot of questions. We better get going. I have a ton of work to do."

Startled by the change in his tone and his brusque behavior, Bella observed the tight muscles in his back as he went to the horses, untying Galahad and whistling to Calico, who immediately came to his side.

"What's wrong?" she asked.

"Nothing. Just lost track of time. You ready?"

"Of course." She ignored his outstretched hand, grabbed hold of the pommel, and mounted Galahad without his assistance.

THEY RODE BACK IN SILENCE, Bella admiring the scenery and trying to ignore the rude man riding ahead of her. When they neared the end of the trail, Valley Stables came into view. An exhibition was going on with horses from around the area, so the grassy parking lots near the tracks were full and spectators lined the fences. Whip skirted the tracks and led her behind the stables. As they passed the complex and headed down the hill, Tom spied them. He'd just emerged from showing the stables to a group of clients. Whip tipped his hat and his sister waved, but they didn't stop.

Hmm...what's the matter with those two? Tom thought, watching them. *Just as well.* He liked and respected Whip, but wasn't crazy about him becoming too chummy with his sister. He knew his assistant had a troubled past, but had never asked for details.

OUTSIDE THE BARN, Bella dismounted and turned to him. "Shall I groom him here or take him up to the stables?"

Whip pushed his hat back, scratching his forehead as he looked over at Galahad. "He'll stay here with us for the day, but one of the guys can do it after they finish the stalls."

"I owe you an hour's work, remember?"

"Not necessary, but thanks anyway."

"Well, I say it is!" she replied a bit more stridently than she intended. "I'll brush him down, put him out, and see if they need help with the stalls. That should keep me busy." With that, she turned on her heel and stomped off, leading Galahad into the barn. Once inside, she realized she had no idea where to get curry brushes, buckets, or water. Fortunately, she ran into Greg with a wheelbarrow of dirty hay.

"Hey, Greg, where should I cool Galahad down?"

Greg had a huge shit-eating grin on his face, and she wondered if he'd observed their little scene.

"You can use the stall at the end. All cleaned. There are brushes in a bucket. The hose is right there too."

"Thanks," she said, refusing to meet his gaze or look back in the direction she'd come.

An hour later, covered with hay and dust, Bella admired the three stalls she'd mucked out. Whip and Greg were nowhere to be seen, and the other two guys who'd been mucking alongside her had also disappeared. She paused, and the stillness of the barn enveloped her, the sweet smell of fresh hay comforting. After a few minutes, she stowed her pitchfork and headed up to the house for a shower.

CHAPTER 3

When Whip walked by the farmhouse, he noticed that Bella's old blue Highlander was gone. He realized he'd been a jerk, but the mention of siblings had touched a nerve and a part of his past that he wasn't prepared to open. He carried photos of Johnny and Ellie in his wallet and looked at them every morning and every night, but he sure as hell wasn't ready to talk about them.

Suddenly, he heard clip-clopping behind him and turned to find his boss on a tall gray Trakehner. Like Galahad, Blue had been bought for stud, to support their nascent dressage program. Blue had been a spirited, fierce competitor, but was now retired. Tom's favorite, most people assumed that the beautiful warm-blood belonged to him since they were always together.

Tom pulled up alongside him. "Good ride?"

"Nice morning for it."

Tom hopped off the horse and confronted him. "Not what I asked."

"All you're gonna get."

"What happened? Did she do something?"

"I'm just not great at babysitting novice riders."

Wrong answer. Tom's eyes narrowed. "You know damn well my

sister's as competent a rider as you or me. Now what the hell happened?"

"Nothing, boss. I'm just having a crap morning."

"Because?"

"Because I'm me. Dark moods sometimes happen to me. Nothing to do with Bella."

"You want to talk about it?"

"Nope."

"Okay, fine." Tom mounted Blue. "But I'm here anytime. I'm no shrink, but I'm a pretty good listener."

"Thanks, boss."

Whip watched Tom ride off. "Shit, shit, shit," he muttered under his breath as he headed down the hill to say hello to Tom's fiancée, Grace, who was in the first of two round pens working with Dusty.

BELLA ARRIVED Valley Ob-Gyn twenty minutes before her first patient, Ruthie Morgan Langdon. One of her bosses, Dr. Marc Koenig, met her in the hall on her way to her office. "I smell horse," he said.

Bella's face dropped. "You're kidding! I took a long shower."

The tall, thin senior physician pushed sandy hair back from his forehead as he grinned at her. "Haven't you heard? I have super olfactory powers."

"No, I hadn't heard."

"Early morning ride?"

"Yup."

"Lucky you. I get out when I can, but my poor old Skip doesn't get near enough exercise these days."

"You have a horse?"

"Three, actually. My daughters ride competitively."

"Why did I not know this?"

He chuckled. "I like to think I have a few secrets."

"Where do you keep them? The horses, I mean."

"We board them at Morgan's Run now, but I'm on the waiting list at Valley Stables. My girls do dressage, and it would help to have them there for lessons and training. I mean, Maggie and her crew are terrific, but it's probably the logical next step. It was actually Maggie who suggested it."

"Did you know I live out there with my brother?"

"Yes, which is one of the reasons I've never mentioned it to you. Don't want any favors. I've brought up Maisie and Julie to stand on their own merits. It's something that was really important to their mom."

"Good for you. So important," Bella said, noticing that tears rimmed his blue eyes.

"Well... I won't keep you. Have a good day," he said, nodding as he turned away.

"Thanks. You too," she said.

"Hey, Jacobi," he called as she reached her office door. "Ignore the horse-smell comment. I actually like it."

She sat at her desk, pondering the interaction. *Was he flirting with me?* she wondered as she shuffled through the files for her afternoon appointments and powered up her computer on the cart beside the desk. She knew Marc had lost his wife, Bonnie, a year earlier after her long battle with cancer. She also knew he had kids, but not much else. For the two months she'd been at Valley Ob-Gyn, she'd kept her head down and worked hard, with little time for office gossip. After her last job in Montana, she preferred to keep her distance at work.

She'd become friends with Gretchen Sullivan, one of her fellow midwives, but otherwise, she socialized with townspeople. She'd joined Valley Chorus and the Scrabble Club, both of which Grace, her brother's fiancée, and Aria Firorelli, Spark Foster's chef, were regular attendees. Spark was one of the owners of Valley Stables. Grace and Tom encouraged her to come to Scrabble Night, and Aria had nagged until Bella agreed to try the chorus. She'd joined only a few weeks earlier, but she loved it.

Suzie Breen, one of the practice's physician assistants, popped her head in the door. "Hey, Bella, your one o'clock's here. I've put her in room two."

"Thanks, Suz. Be right there."

Bella stood, stretched, then grabbed Ruthie's file, tucking it under her arm. She draped her stethoscope around her shoulders and wheeled the computer cart out the door. *Feels like an appointment with the Queen Mother*, she thought as she knocked on the door of Examining Room Two. Wife of Tom's boss, Harley Langdon, Ruthie was here for her three-month post-birth checkup. Bella opened the door to find her patient perched at the end of the table, texting on her phone.

"Hi, Ruthie."

"Hi, Bella." Immediately, the petite redhead with freckles and pale blue eyes tossed her phone atop her pile of clothes lying in a jumble on a nearby chair. "Long time no see."

"Not too long," Bella said, smiling. "How are you?"

"Great. A little irritation at the site where I tore, but I've been taking lots of baths, and Harley's been real gentle."

"And how is your beautiful Pickles?"

"She's doing amazingly well. This is her first week at the Cottage, and they say she's settled in like a champ. My mom and Carmela are having baby withdrawal, but they'll get over it. Besides, there are plenty more babies for them to fuss over."

"You're so lucky to have the Cottage and so much support."

The Cottage was a day care and nursery built, staffed, and financed by the elder Morgans and their dear friend Spark Foster. Free and open to all children of their employees and, of course, their grandchildren, it was a lovely light-filled space with a well-equipped school and playground.

Most Morgan grandchildren spent their first months at the Big House with Granny Leonora and her housekeeper, Carmela. Carmela and her husband, Raoul, manager of the ranch's livestock, had never been blessed with children of their own, but had raised many Morgan offspring over the years. Penelope "Pickles" Langdon had been with her grandmother and Carmela, along with baby Cora, Maggie and Ben's third. Cora, who traveled between the Big House at

Morgan's Run and Maggie's dad's in town, was still a few weeks away from joining the Cottage crew.

"We sure are."

Bella pulled the computer cart close and sat beside Ruthie. "Looks like all your vitals are great. Let's just take a quick peek and then we can chat in my office. Sound okay?"

Bella called Suzie in.

"Everything looks great," she said a few minutes later as she completed her examination and handed Ruthie her clothes. "I'll see you when you're ready, okay?"

Bella went to her office, typed up her notes from the exam and grabbed two waters from the cabinet. She had a rule—no computer work with the patient. Thus, she scheduled extra time to enter notes into the electronic files after the examination or before her next patient.

When Ruthie joined her a few minutes later, she pushed the computer cart aside and came around the desk to sit beside her on one of two office chairs. "So, you're in good shape and have healed well. I asked Suzie to grab samples of a cream you can put on your scar, and I'll phone a prescription into the pharmacy, just in case you want more. I'd suggest using it at least twice a day, but definitely after you wash and before and after intercourse."

"Thanks."

"They'll be at the desk when you check out. Now, what questions do you have for me?"

"Not many. Do I just return now to a yearly checkup."

"Yes, but if you have any concerns or questions, be sure to call or make an appointment before then. How's the nursing going?"

"You mean the pump-nurse, pump-nurse till my boobs feel like they're gonna fall off?"

"Are they sore?"

"No, they're fine. I use lanolin when needed. Pickles is a trooper. She latched on and has never let go. She transitions really well between bottle and breast, thank God."

"Good baby."

"So how are you settling in, Bella? Is Valley life suiting you?"

"I love it. Such beautiful country, and the people are so friendly. Most people, that is."

Antennae up, Ruthie eyed her. "Oh? Have you had trouble with someone?"

Bella smiled, waving her hands. "No, just a weird episode with Whip Kittredge this morning. My brother wouldn't let me ride alone, so he assigned Whip to babysit me."

"Smart, with all the cougar sightings lately. So what happened?"

"Everything was going great, then he just clammed up, turned stone cold, and stayed that way for the rest of the ride. It was very strange."

"No trigger?"

"We were talking about his family, and I asked about brothers and sisters, and *boom*, that was it."

"Hmm, I don't know Whip that well. I mean he's a great guy and I know Harley and Tom depend on him to keep the other guys in line, but I don't think anyone knows much about his past. I can ask Harley?"

"No, please don't. He was probably just in a bad mood. I certainly don't want to cause trouble."

"Okay, but I'll keep my radar up. By the way, we're having our Friday-night barbecue this week. I hope you and Tom are coming?"

"He hasn't mentioned it, but I'm sure we'll be there. Thanks."

They chatted for a few more minutes, then Ruthie said goodbye just as Suzie popped in to announce Bella's next patient. Bella decided to put Whip Kittredge and his moods out of her mind as she gathered her notes and headed in to greet a very pregnant Amy Barnes, daughter of Spark Foster. Her husband, Jeb, a wrangler working at Morgan's Run, was with her. Amy was due any minute.

CHAPTER 4

"Leave it alone, sis. That's my advice. Whip's a real private person, and we need to respect that," Tom said as brother and sister ate dinner on the back terrace. It was a warm night, and Bella had grilled chicken, which she served with several salads. "This rice salad is fantastic, by the way."

"It's faro, actually. Better for us."

He grinned. "I liked it better when I thought it was rice."

"Ha-ha. So...of course, I'll leave it alone, but it was really odd, you know? One minute, we were having a nice ride, chatting and all, and the next, he shut down with barely a word."

Tom shrugged. "Change of subject. Ruthie and Harley are having a barbecue Friday. You want to go?"

"Yup. Are you coming to Scrabble tonight?"

"No. much as I love you and Grace, I'm beat. I've gotta get up before dawn tomorrow. New arrivals, and then I've gotta hustle back here for the trainer comin' about Ghost. He's arriving at eight along with Nick Parker. We're hoping he'll give us some pointers. If Ghost doesn't settle soon, the big bosses are going sell him."

"You mean ship him off for slaughter? You can't let them do that!"

"They're in charge, not me. Besides, he's dangerous. To the other horses, not to mention people."

"Poor guy."

"Yeah, he's an incredible animal."

"Why couldn't they just set him free?"

"That's one solution, but we've got his herd, and unless they truck him hundreds of miles away, he'll find his way back."

Bella ate the last bite of dinner, then stood, placing her plate in the sink. "I'm off. You crash. Leave everything, and I'll clean up after Scrabble."

WHIP AND GREG decided to grab a burger at the Bulldog Saloon in town. A couple of the crew joined them, and they sat at a back booth with a pitcher of Desert Amber, the local brew. All ordered Bulldog Burgers, the bar's most popular entrée. As the guys talked, Whip sat back, half listening, mostly thinking about the morning's ride with Bella. *Idiot*, he thought, sipping his beer. His companions were on their second and third mugs, but he had barely touched his. Truth was, even though he could act like the life of any party, he rarely drank more than one drink.

Noting his uncharacteristic silence, Greg asked, "You okay, boss?"

He gave him a wry smile. "Sort of. I was an asshole earlier today, and I'm trying to think of how to make up for it."

"Wanna talk about it?"

"Nope."

"Okay, then. Here's our burgers," Greg said as Jackie, the waitress, set huge platters of burgers and curly fries in front of them.

GRACE PUSHED locks of sandy hair from her eyes, hazel eyes twinkling. "Want to grab a nightcap?" she asked as she and Bella stacked chairs and tables at the end of Scrabble. Her brother's fiancée was lovely, slim, and delicate in faded jeans and a light gray McGraw's Hardware sweatshirt. Bella looked over at her in surprise.

"I know, I know… Doesn't sound like me, but I'm pretty sure I'll find my dad at the Bulldog, and maybe I can drag him home before he passes out on the bar."

"Of course. Love a nightcap," Bella said, "Everything's cleaned up. Shall we?"

THE DARK SALOON, its walls covered with black-and-white photos of cowboys and rodeos, was relatively quiet. A few men sat at the bar, including Wilbur McGraw, and there were half a dozen occupied booths, no one in the two back rooms on a Wednesday night. "There's the perpetrator," Grace said, as they spied Wilbur McGraw chatting with several men at the far end of the bar. "He looks fine, so let's have one drink down here, then I'll take him home."

"Don't you want to say hi?" Bella asked as she gazed behind Grace's dad to the booths. The men's backs were to them, but she was ninety-nine percent certain Whip was with the group in the back booth.

"No, I'd rather he not know I'm here. That way, I can observe his condition."

"What?" Bella said, realizing she hadn't heard her friend.

"Do you see someone you'd rather avoid?" Grace asked, noticing her companion's expression.

"Maybe…yes. I had a weird interaction with one of the guys this morning."

"Oh?"

"Do you know much about Whip?"

"No, but I think he's gorgeous in a Wild West outlaw kind of way."

Bella nodded. "Yeah, he's cute all right, but also an enigma. One minute, he's warm and friendly, the next, he's like a stone."

"He's always been friendly to me, but then, I don't know him well. Did you ask your brother?"

"Yes, and he said Whip had a troubled past, but he doesn't know what happened. Says he can be moody."

"Aren't they all? Except for Tom, of course." Grace smiled, a dreamy look in her eyes.

"Oh, he has his moments, but you're right. He's pretty steady. I'm glad you two found each other."

"Me too."

They chatted while sipping their wine until Grace said, "It's time. Gotta get him home before I have to beg for someone to help me."

They had walked from the Community Center, so Bella's car was still there. Since their route took them by the hardware store, McGraw's house behind it, Bella said, "I'll walk with you."

Grace tapped her father's shoulder just as the crew from Valley Stables strolled up to settle their bill.

"Hey, Grace," Whip said, then noticed her companion. "Bella."

"Hi, we just stopped in for a drink after Scrabble."

"Great," he said, distracted by the father-daughter squabble going on beside them.

"Not ready," Wilbur said, shoving Grace's arm aside.

"Yes, you are, Dad. Come on." Hazel eyes reflecting her exasperation, Grace looked over at Russ Keeler, the saloon owner, who stood behind the bar.

"Last call, Wilbur. Out you go," Russ said. "Escort your beautiful daughter home now."

McGraw set his empty glass down sharply. "I'm ready for another, Russ."

Suddenly, Whip pivoted and got in the man's face. "Hey, Wilbur, what's up? We're just heading out, and I wanted to talk with you about a pickup tomorrow. Walk with me, buddy." He didn't wait for an answer, but instead took hold of McGraw's arm and pulled him to his feet. Miraculously, Wilbur followed without a peep. Whip winked at Grace over her father's shoulder, and they walked out, each holding one of Wilbur's arms. Behind her father's back, she mouthed a silent *thank you*.

Greg and the others followed the entourage up the street, Bella behind them. Whip carried on a nonstop conversation about tools and supplies until they reached the McGraws' front door.

As they climbed the porch, the situation well in hand, Bella called, "Night!" to Grace and turned to walk the short distance to her car.

Whip helped Grace inside and hurried back out. Greg and the others were there, but no one else. "She's gone, boss," Greg said. "Her car's parked at the Community Center."

Whip shrugged. "Okay, let's go home."

CHAPTER 5

Thursday morning, after taking most of the horses out of the barn, Tom and Whip met Bobby Chavos, a trainer and so-called horse whisperer from Prescott. Bobby arrived at the same time as their resident whisperer, Nick Parker. Earlier, Tom made the decision to have Whip work with Nick and Bobby. "Ghost is your project, buddy," he said. "This is his last chance. Remember, if there's no improvement, we're gonna have to cut him loose."

"What's that mean?" Whip asked, knowing full well what Tom meant.

"Let's not worry about that now. Here they come. Morning!" He strode toward the men, extending his hand to the trainer. "Mr. Chavos welcome. "I'm Tom Jacobi, and this is Whip Kittredge, my assistant. I've put him in charge of the Ghost project, along with you and our local horse whisperer, Nick Parker."

"It's Bobby, man," the burly man with dark hair and deeply tanned skin said.

They all shook hands, then Tom said, "Ghost is in the big round pen. Shall we?" As they walked, he said, "I forgot to ask. Are you commuting from Prescott the next couple of weeks, or do you need a place here?"

"My sister lives in town. I'm staying with her," Bobby said as they reached the pen.

The four men stood outside the fence observing the white stallion. Unsettled by their presence, Ghost pawed the ground and snorted.

Bobby whistled. "He's a beaut."

"That he is," Tom said. "So, what's the plan?"

"We three will go in nice and slow. Initially, I'll work with him with Nick's assistance and Whip will mirror our actions, gradually taking over in the coming days while we slowly step back. Sound good?"

Whip chuckled. "All except the part where we go in there."

"You're afraid? That's good," the trainer said. "You'll need that fear to channel your energy and keep you sharp. From this moment on, that guy pawing the ground is no longer in charge."

"You gonna use that Aussie stick in there?" Nick asked indicating the training tool in Bobby's hand.

"Only when I need to. I'm not a big fan of these, but going into a round pen with the likes of that brute, I'd be a fool not to have it with me. You ready?"

They walked toward the gate as Tom hung back, watching Ghost, nostrils flared, ears pinned back as he followed their every move. "Careful guys. At the first sign of trouble, jump the fence."

As the men slipped through the gate into the pen, the stallion tossed his head back, whinnying and snorting. Bobby began making soft clicking sounds in response. Nick echoed him as they began circling the edge of the pen. Ghost's eyes never left them as they slowly made their way around. They had almost completed the circuit when the horse reared up and charged.

"Stand your ground," Bobby said, "Get behind me, but stand your ground." As the horse reached him, he raised the stick, flicking the attached rope.

"Hey, boy, you're okay," he said softly, his feet planted on the dusty ground, not yielding an inch.

After a chorus of snorts and hooves pounding the ground, the stallion turned and retreated to the opposite end of the pen. Nick whistled softly. "He's coming back, you know."

"Oh yeah," Bobby said. "This is only the beginning."

Tom watched the dance between horse and wranglers for a few minutes, then wished them good luck and headed up the hill to the stables. Whip stood alongside Nick, but both men deferred to Bobby, who appeared to be locked in an epic battle with Ghost.

BELLA HAD JUST RETURNED from lunch with a fellow midwife when a call buzzed on her cell. "Hey, Bella, this is Jeb. It's happening, she's in labor." His voice sounded as if he were in a wind tunnel.

"Where are you?" she asked, sprinting down the hall to her office to get her bag and birthing duffel.

"On the Gila about ten miles from town. Spark just called. He and Aria are with her at his place."

"I'm on my way," Bella said, clicking off.

Spark Foster's estate sat at the western edge of the Valley about five miles southwest of town. He'd purchased the property from Ben and Leonora Morgan and built a huge main house and several barns and outbuildings. There was also acreage enough for his son and daughter to build homes if they chose. Buck, his eldest, lived in Laguna Beach, California, and appeared to have no inclination to settle in the Valley. He and Amy had grown up in Portland, Oregon, and he still considered that home. On the other hand, his younger sister loved the Valley, and she and Jeb were excited about eventually building on the property.

Bella turned down the long drive that led to the sprawling estate, marveling at what wealth could accomplish. A self-made billionaire, Spark made his fortune in alternative energy technologies and had companies and contracts all over the world.

The man himself was waiting at the open door as she pulled up, his normally calm demeanor in absentia. He rushed down to the car and grabbed the duffel. "Hey, darlin', thank the Lord you're here! Went through this with my Patty, but that was many years ago."

"How's she doing?" Bella asked as she walked beside the tall, robust sixty-something. Over the years, Spark had sometimes been mistaken for Fred Thompson, the actor and politician. Today, Fred appeared to be coming unglued.

"My little girl's strong, but she'll be happy to see you and Jeb, when he gets here."

Bella followed him upstairs to a large light-filled room in the house's west wing. Part of a suite of rooms Spark had designed with Amy in mind, there was a sitting room, three bedrooms, and two baths. When Amy and Jeb adopted their wheelchair-bound son, Toby, Jeb had also installed an elevator at the far end of the hall.

Bella hurried through the sitting room and stepped into the largest bedroom, where Amy sat on a large blue exercise ball, gently bouncing.

"Oh Bella! So glad you're here." Amy brushed hair from her damp cheeks and gave her a wan smile. Aria Firorelli, Spark's chef, stood nearby holding a damp facecloth.

"Hey, is that bouncing working for you?" Bella asked, setting down her bag and directing Spark to place the duffel near the bed.

"Yes, I think so."

"Because you can rest, or even get in the tub if that's more comfortable."

Amy continued to bounce as a contraction began. "Ow, ah, ee," she keened, pain evident on her face.

After a quick hug, Bella went to the bed to set up her materials. She asked Aria for a table, and the chef pulled a square table to the side of the bed, covering it with a towel. Bella spread a waterproof cover over the bed, then her soft birthing blankets. She then laid out on the table sterile gloves, gauze pads, thermometer, and a cotton cap for the baby. She set a sitz pan aside for after the birth and a small oxygen tank, should the baby need it. Finally, she set up a collapsible IV stand in case Amy became dehydrated or needed nourishment.

Setting up took less than five minutes, during which time Spark held his daughter's hand, encouraging her until a contraction eased.

Stethoscope around her neck, she turned to Amy and Spark. "How far apart do they seem?"

"Oh gee, darlin' I'm not sure."

"About five minutes," Aria said.

"Okay, then," Bella said, just as footsteps sounded on the stairs and Jeb Barnes burst into the room. Short, with the wiry, strong build of a wrangler, Jeb tossed his baseball cap on the chair and ran his hand through his brownish-red hair. Grayish-blue eyes full of concern, he rushed to his wife's side. "How are you baby?"

Amy wrapped her arms around his strong shoulders. "Oh Jeb, I want this to be over!"

"Course you do," he said, looking over at Bella. "What's going on?"

"So glad you're here, Dad. I was just going get her to the bed so I can check."

Without a word, he swooped Amy up. Cradling her in his arms, he whispered, "I've got you, baby." He carried her to the king-size bed, kissed her on the forehead, then gently laid her down.

Aria handed him the facecloth, which he applied to Amy's brow as another contraction began. "Breathe, baby," he said, holding her face and gazing into her eyes.

"Oh gosh, your breath!" Amy cried. "What the hell did you have for lunch?"

"Burritos. Sorry, babe. Want me to go in and brush my teeth real quick?"

"Don't you dare!" Her fingers dug into his shoulders as they breathed together through the pain.

As the contraction subsided, Amy gazed around the room. "Who's getting Toby? He'll be waiting at school."

"No worries, darlin'," her father said. "Ned's picking him up along with Emma. He's gotta swing by the Cottage for Bennie, but then he'll bring Toby here."

A few minutes later, Bella completed her examination and looked up at Jeb. "She's fully dilated. I'm gonna ask her to push with the next contraction and it will be easier if she's partially sitting up."

Jeb slipped out of his boots and eased himself behind his wife, his back against the headboard, arms around her. "Here we go, baby."

Four contractions later, Jeb held a perfect baby boy in his arms before handing him to Amy. "Hi, sweet boy," she whispered, tears in her eyes.

Bella smiled as she completed her post-birth exam. *It never gets old*, she mused, watching the young couple.

Spark and Aria had stepped out to give them privacy during the delivery. Now he knocked, then popped his head around the door. "Did I hear someone new in here?"

"It's a boy, Daddy," Amy said, tears streaming down her cheeks. "Come see him! We're calling him Spencer Jake Barnes after both his grandfathers." Spencer was Spark's first name, seldom used, and Jeb's father was Jake.

Amy handed the baby to her father. Tears in his eyes, Spark gazed down at the infant. "Well, now, poor little fella with a name like that. He sure is cute. We'll have to think up a nickname. Can't have him goin' through life as Spencer."

CHAPTER 6

Friday afternoon, Bella walked down to the barn to find her brother. She'd worked that morning, but taken the afternoon off. Birthing babies, particularly when she did it solo as she had the previous afternoon, always took a lot out of her, and she was exhausted. She smiled, thinking of little Spencer in his parents' arms. *What a sweetie, with his full head of red hair.* She rounded the barn and spied Tom in the round pen with three others, Whip, Nick Parker, and a tall, dark-skinned stranger. *The horse whisperer.* Miraculously, they had managed to get a soft harness and lunge line on Ghost, but he clearly didn't like it.

Tom turned and waved at her, coming to the edge of the fence. "Hey, sis."

"How'd you ever get that gear on him?"

"Nick's harness. He somehow got him into it in the stall this morning, but even though it's real soft, it's been a major distraction. Old Ghosty is a stubborn one."

No sooner were the words out of his mouth than Ghost charged, headed straight for brother and sister. "Tom!" she cried as he leapt over the fence, just escaping the stallion's raised hooves.

"Bastard," he muttered, brushing dust from his jeans.

The stranger clucked at the horse, then said, "He don't like talkin', unless it's directed at him."

"Well, I'm done for the day and you should be too. Bobby this is my sister Bella."

"Hey," the man said, tipping his hat.

Acutely aware of Whip beside him, Bella said hello, then nodded to his two companions, quickly directing her attention back to Tom. "You ready?"

"Yup." He turned to the men. "I'm gonna suggest you quit now. Whip can take him in after he calms down. Bobby, you're welcome to come to Harley's tonight for supper. Nick too. It'll be most of the crew from here."

"Thanks, but I'm goin' to a family thing with my sister," the trainer replied, his eyes never leaving the stallion, now snorting and pawing the ground at the far side of the pen.

"Night, then. Will we see you tomorrow?"

"Half day. I'll be over around one."

Brother and sister waved, turning to walk back through the barn and up the hill to the farmhouse. "Looks like Ghost is giving them a run for their money," she said.

Tom shrugged. "Kind of nightmare, but it's only been a couple of days. Some horses never get there."

"He's sure worth it, though, right?"

"Maybe. Do I want to know what's up with you and Kittredge?"

"No...and there's nothing up."

"Except tension you can cut with a knife."

Bella rolled he eyes. "Is that even an expression?"

He laughed. "Darned if I know."

"I'm going to pop in the shower and I'll be ready to go in fifteen," she said as they climbed the front porch.

"Me too."

∼

WHIP WALKED INTO THE LANGDONS' as most people were loading plates with burgers, steaks, and all manner of side dishes and salads. He stopped to say hi to Willow, Harley's daughter, a sophomore at University of Arizona in Tucson. Willow's mom, Talia, and Harley had dated in college, then split up. Unbeknownst to him, she'd left school pregnant with his child and raised Willow on her own. Several years ago, Talia had contacted Harley because she was dying. After her mom's passing, Willow moved to the Valley to live with Ruthie and her dad.

"Hey, Willow," he said, kneeling beside her and baby Pickles. "Home for the weekend?"

She smiled at him, her eyes dreamy. "It's spring break actually."

Whip knew she had a crush on him, but also knew if he made a move, her father would tar and feather him. She was a sweetheart, but way too young. *And she isn't Bella Jacobi*, he thought, surprised by that train of thought. *Talk about people who'd tar and feather me. Tom might actually skin me alive.* "Good deal. You doing anything special?"

"Two of my friends are staying for the week. We're going on a short pack trip."

"Yeah? By yourselves?"

She laughed. "No way. Not with all the cougar sightings and everything. We're going east, which, apparently, they think is safer. A couple of Uncle Robbie's guys are taking us, and Dad's footing the bill." Ruthie's brother Robbie ran an adventure tours company based in Saguaro.

"Lucky you."

"Yeah."

"Hey, Pickles," he said tickling the baby under the chin. Ruthie and Harley's youngest daughter giggled and reached her hands out.

"She likes you," Willow said.

"And I like her, don't I, Pickles? Hey, why don't you get food and hang with your friends? I'll keep her for a while."

"Really?"

"Go!"

Whip headed across the lawn, meeting up with Greg and some of the guys, who alternately teased him for carrying a baby or when he baby-talked at Pickles. As he stood talking with them, he glanced upward to the magnificent home's wide third-floor porch, where Harley manned the grill and guests carried plates groaning with food to tables on each deck or on the grass, where a half dozen picnic tables sat at various spots.

"Be careful of my baby!" Ruthie called from above, two platters of food in her arms.

Whip gave her a thumbs-up, then turned to spy Tom, Bella, and Grace sitting in the shade with Ben and Maggie Morgan. Emma Morgan was nearby on a blanket, helping feed Charlotte, Pickles's two-and-a-half-year-old sister. Her cousin, Cora, a few weeks younger than Pickles, slept in a basket beside them. Charlotte appeared to be putting more food in her lap than her mouth. Maggie hopped up to assist her daughter.

"Hey, Kittredge," Ben Morgan called. "Bring my niece over here and join us."

As soon as he reached the table, Ben grabbed the baby, swinging her up over his head. "Hey, Pickie!"

"Ben, be careful of her neck!" Maggie called, her capris now covered in ketchup.

"She's fine babe," he said, cradling his niece as he looked over at Whip. "How'd you end up babysitting?"

"Giving Willow a break so she can eat with her buddies."

"Why don't you go grab some grub? We'll keep her. Pickie's used to being passed around, aren't you, baby?"

"Thanks, I will," Whip said. As he headed for the porch stairs, he nodded to Bella and Tom. His boss tipped his hat, while his sister looked like she'd swallowed a cactus.

As Whip filled his plate at the buffet, Ruthie caught up with him. "What have you done with my baby?"

"Her Uncle Ben has her."

"Oh Lord, I'd better get down there. No telling where she'll end up next!"

Whip's face fell. "Jeez, I'm sorry. I thought with three kids, he was—"

She smiled, squeezing his forearm. "I'm kidding. She's fine. With Maggie supervising, my stupid brother can't get into too much trouble."

BELLA OBSERVED every movement Whip made as he interacted with people on the porch. She'd been amazed to see him with Pickles and the gentle way he handled the infant. Now as he descended the steps with a plate of food and beer, he was chatting with Ruthie, her arm linked through his. As they neared the table, Bella turned away, realizing that Grace had been talking to her and she hadn't heard a word.

"I'm sorry, I was in dreamland," she said, smiling at her brother's fiancée, with whom she'd become good friends in the past few months.

Grace gave her a knowing smile. "He is pretty dreamy," Grace whispered, not softly enough to escape Tom's notice.

"Who's dreamy?" he asked.

Grace patted his arm. "We were saying the burger sauce is so creamy."

Tom eyed her, shaking his head. "Bullshit, but I know better than to try to pry secrets out of you two."

"Hey, Shortcake," Ben said, rocking the baby in his arms. "We've been having a good time, haven't we, Pickie?"

Ruthie gently took the baby from him. "Do not call me Shortcake, especially in front of my children, and I absolutely forbid you to call Pickles Pickie!"

"Aw, you know how I love a good nickname, sis."

"Ha-ha!" She rolled her eyes, gazing over at Whip, who stood at the end of the table.

"Okay if I join you?" he asked.

Ben clapped him on the shoulder. "We invited you, man. Besides,

I want to hear all about this new guy, the horse whisperer who's working with the stallion. Nick says he's amazing."

"He is, but Ghost is tough."

They spent the next half hour discussing the merits of various training approaches. Grace and Bella joined Maggie and Ruthie on the blanket. "I don't know how you do it all day, Maggie," Bella said.

"Oh?"

"The wrangler talk."

Maggie smiled her glorious smile that stopped men dead in their tracks. "I have to admit, I love it, but I love horses, all horses."

"With you and your Tabasco, I guess so," Bella said. She referred to the enormous draft horse they had gentled from one of their first shipments of wild horses. Originally intended for the border patrol program, Tabasco had scared off every potential rider because of his size. He now lived at Maggie and Ben's. He was her horse, and gentle as he was, few people dared ride him.

"I do hope they can settle Ghost down. He's a beautiful horse. It would be a shame if we...they had to give him up," Maggie said.

The Langdon barbecues usually ended around nine. As Bella walked out with Tom and Grace, she veered off to say thanks to Ruthie and also to catch up with Aria and to check on Amy.

"She's doing great," Spark's chef said, her handsome, dark-haired boyfriend, Jonas Miller, by her side. Jonas was an East Coast transplant, an engineer who had come west to work for Spark.

"I'll stop by tomorrow to check on her," Bella said. "Night."

As she turned away, she bumped smack into Whip, who appeared to be waiting to speak to either herself or her companions. He nodded to the couple, then turned to her.

"Got a minute?"

Shaken by his nearness, she swallowed hard. "Just. I came with Tom and Grace, and they're waiting."

"I just wanted to apologize for the other day. I was an asshole, and I'm really sorry."

She nodded. "Thanks. It was just confusing."

"I'm sure. Well... I just wanted to... I mean I wondered if you'd have dinner with me sometime. To make up for my rudeness?"

Shocked, she stared at him.

"I guess that's a no," he said after several long seconds elapsed.

"No... I mean, I'm just surprised. But sure, I'd like to have dinner. When?" His nearness unnerved her, yet she felt drawn to him like a moth to a flame. *I could get lost in those smoky-gray eyes.*

"Whenever you're free. Tomorrow night?"

"Tomorrow's fine," she said as Whip grinned.

"Great."

"Did you have a place in mind? I mean just so I know how to dress."

"I was thinking Vermillion. Have you been there?"

"No, but I hear it's wonderful."

"It's pretty good. Also, not fancy, so you can dress any way you want."

"Okay, then," she said, wondering if the conversation they were having was real. "What time?"

"Pick you up at seven, unless your brother freaks out and doesn't let you go."

"My brother is not my keeper. See you then," she said. "Night."

His expression unreadable as she turned away, Bella realized she'd been holding her breath. She let it out in a whoosh as she hurried to find Tom and Grace.

CHAPTER 7

"You're what?" Tom asked as brother and sister ate breakfast together the next morning. Bella had made omelets loaded with mushrooms, pepper, onions, and local cheese, which she served with crispy Morgan's Run bacon and her brother's favorite lumberjack hashbrowns.

"It's just dinner. He felt bad about being such an asshole on the ride, so he wants to make up for it."

"A simple, 'sorry I was a jerk' would have done the trick. Dinner? Come on, sis."

"What's the matter with you?"

"I just don't think Whip's the best thing for you. You've barely gotten over Derek the sleazeball."

"Yes, I have."

"Kittredge is a bit of a loose cannon."

"In what way?"

"I don't know. That's what bothers me."

Bella stood and cleared their plates. "It's just dinner."

He eyed her over his reading glasses. "It's never just dinner."

"Well, this is," she said as she rinsed the dishes and loaded the dishwasher. "I love these dish drawers," she added, referring to the two-drawer stainless steel dishwasher. "If I ever get a place of my own, I'm going to get these."

"Mega bucks, but don't change the subject."

She came and sat beside him. "There is no subject. I'm having dinner with one of the ranch guys. Period, end of story."

"Where are you going anyway?"

"Vermillion. I've been wanting to try that."

Tom threw up his hands. "I rest my case. Vermillion? Now I know it's more than dinner!"

"You're being ridiculous, brother dear. You know that, don't you?"

"It's my job to be ridiculous, to look after you."

"No, it is not. Yet another reason for me to get my own place. Then you wouldn't know what I was doing."

He looked at her, surprised. "You're not looking, are you?"

"No, I love it out here, but I can start. You and Grace are going to want your privacy soon. What married woman wants her sister-in-law sharing her house?"

"Well, there's no hurry. We're taking things slow till she gets her dad in better shape." In his grief over losing his wife, Wilbur McGraw, Grace's dad, had begun drinking heavily, and it was a constant worry for his daughter.

"What are you guys doing tonight?"

"Movies in Grenville and maybe dinner. Now I'm thinking I should suggest we go out to Vermillion. She loves it there."

"Ha-ha," she said, throwing her napkin at him.

"Okay, okay. What are you up to today?"

"Grocery shopping, since we have no food in the fridge, then I'm going to clean this filthy place from top to bottom. Want me to wash your sheets and towels?"

"You don't have to do that."

"I'm happy to."

"Okay, thanks. Knock yourself out."

They went through this same ritual every week. Bella considered cleaning, cooking, and laundry to be her rent. While Tom didn't agree about the rent part, he always acquiesced in the end and was greatly appreciative.

"Where'll you be, up or down?" she asked.

"Mostly up with today's exhibition. The big bosses are keyed to show off the place to a bunch of high rollers. I think they're looking for investors. The crew's all set down here. Grace is coming to work with Dusty, and we're hoping to grab lunch."

"Oh gee, you don't want me running around with the vacuum during your lunch, do you?"

"Very funny. If we even have lunch, it'll be up at the stables. We'll grab something off the buffet they're setting out."

"Maybe I'll stroll down and watch Grace and Dusty for a while. She's done wonders with him, hasn't she?"

"Yup. Bobby's coming to work with Ghost, Nick too, as well as your boyfriend."

"Ha-ha."

"Thanks, for breakfast, Belle. Probably see you later?"

"Not if I see you first," she called as he headed down the hall. *Boyfriend indeed!*

"MORNING, GRACE," Whip called as Tom's fiancée emerged from the barn.

"Hey," she replied, waving.

"Boss has been and gone. He asked me to put Dusty in the corral 'cause we'll be working with Ghost in the round pen."

"Great, thanks. Tom thought if he was doing well, I could ride him up to get lunch. He thought some of the guests might be interested in seeing a Kiger."

"Really?" Whip said. "Is Dusty ready for that?"

The stables had acquired Dusty, a Kiger mustang, along with several other wild horses, including Ghost. All, except for Ghost, were acclimating well and, while not fully gentled, they allowed the saddle and riders under the right circumstances. In other words, capable riders and easy trails. Two of them, quarter horses they'd named Star and Swallow, had come malnourished and in poor health, but you'd never know it now. They'd filled out, and their coats were healthy and shining. The Kiger, Dusty, was the prize of the group, and there was some thought of breeding him with a Kiger that had been bred in captivity. Steady, strong, and gentle, they were a versatile breed popular for riding, cart pulling, and endurance riding. Dusty was considered a Kiger mustang, but the domesticated horses were simply known as Kigers.

Grace shrugged. "Tom's going to decide after asking Harley and the bosses. I hope no one will want to buy him. I'd miss him too much."

"Me too. I've grown pretty attached to the big fella, but I wouldn't worry. Everyone else around here has too. My prediction is that ole Dusty won't be going anywhere in a hurry."

"I hope you're right," she said, turning to head for the corral as Nick and Bobby came to meet Whip. "See ya."

"Let me know if you need help, okay?" he said, then walked down to meet the others.

CHAPTER 8

"What do you think?" Bella asked as she stepped into the living room and twirled in front of Tom. She wore a sleeveless minidress with a swishy skirt and sweetheart neckline, the swirls of the blue-green fabric catching the light in her caramel eyes. Her three-inch espadrilles and the short skirt showcased her slender, shapely legs.

Her brother frowned. "That's not what I call a friendly dinner dress."

"Do you like it? I went to that dress shop in town that everyone raves about. Gabriela's. She has some very cool stuff with not so cool price tags."

"It suits you, and I'm guessing your friendly date will think so too."

"Well, good! Are you getting ready to leave?"

"Not till your boyfriend arrives."

"Oh no, you don't!"

"Oh yes, I do. Don't worry, I'll be cool."

"I'll just bet you will," she said as Whip knocked on the screen door.

Bella grabbed a white shawl and her purse. "All set!" she called, her brother on her heels.

"Hi," Whip said, eyes wide. "You look amazing."

"You too," she said, and he did in black jeans and a blue sport shirt that turned his eyes cerulean. The silver rodeo buckle at his waist looked newly polished, and his usually unruly blond hair had been tamed.

"Hey, Whip," Tom said, stepping out on the porch beside his sister, his arm around her shoulders.

"Hey, boss. You coming along as chaperone?"

"Should I?"

"That depends," Whip said, a huge grin on his face.

"On?"

"On how much you trust your sister and me."

"Oh, I trust her fine. Jury's still out on you."

Bella raised her hands. "That's enough, you two! I have no intention to listen to any more of this ridiculous, chauvinistic nonsense. Good night brother. Hope you and Grace have fun in Grenville." With a backward wave, she headed down the steps to Whip's truck.

"I'm serious," Tom said under his breath.

"I know, and she's fine, boss. No worries."

"Better be. Now, get the hell outta here."

Whip slid into the truck, a grin on his face. "Never seen that over-protective side of the boss."

"Most of it's bluff. Pay no attention."

"Says you," he said. As he started the truck and pulled out of the drive, Tom remained on the porch, arms akimbo. "You don't have to work for the guy."

"The guy's a marshmallow. He's been with me through thick and thin, and he really hates tears."

"What about your folks?"

She shrugged. "They moved to Florida a few years before Tom's divorce. They're very involved in their life down there and weren't around for most of both of our recent ups and downs."

They had reached the Gila Highway, and Whip turned south. "Has moving to the Valley been an up for you?"

"In most ways, yes. I went through a bad breakup. Then a situation with one of my coworkers back home turned into a horror show. It's been great to escape from all that."

She gave him a short account of her stalking coworker at her previous Ob-Gyn practice, but said nothing about Derek and the breakup. Whip listened, but said little except, "Bummer, I'm sorry," at the end of her tale. They rode the remainder of the trip to Vermillion in silence, enjoying the incredible landscape all around them.

The farm-to-table restaurant, so named because of the farm's unusual vermillion-colored soil, was at the end of a long gravel drive-way. At the center of the vast Loggins Farm, the barn-style restaurant was one of several buildings on the property, which included a rambling farmhouse, several barns, sheds, and silos. A meandering arbor behind the house and a couple of other arbors behind the barns grew a variety of grapes used for wine and many of the dishes created by Chef Bissett.

"Wow, this is amazing," Bella said as Whip parked near the restaurant.

"It's a pretty cool place," he said. "I've only been here once when my folks visited last year."

By the time Bella gathered her things, he had rounded the truck and was opening her door. "Thanks," she said, her body grazing his as she stepped out. His scent, sandalwood, and spices, surrounded her as she passed nearer than she'd intended. *Oh my!*

Whip smiled his genuine, beautiful smile. "My pleasure. Shall we?" Hand at the small of her back, he led her toward the entryway.

They were greeted at the door by owner, Edna Loggins, a short round forty-something with rosy cheeks. "Evenin', folks. Welcome!"

Edna seated them by a window that faced northwest. "You'll get a magnificent view of the sunset soon." As they sat down, Edna grabbed a water pitcher and filled their glasses. "Enjoy your meal. Nancy'll be by to take your drinks orders." Edna hurried off toward the door to greet the next arrivals.

Bella gazed across the table at him. "I love this place already."

"Good," he said as a younger version of Edna appeared with menus. "Hey, I'm Nancy. Can I get you something to drink?"

Whip asked for a beer and Bella ordered the house white wine. When Nancy returned, she rattled off the specials, then said, "I'll give you a few minutes."

When Edna's daughter appeared again, they both ordered fish specials, Bella a simple lime-infused trout served with dirty rice and roasted vegetables, and Whip, rainbow trout stuffed with mushrooms, peppers, bacon, and arugula, accompanied by garlic mashed potatoes and grilled asparagus. They asked to split a field greens salad. Nancy pronounced their choices as excellent and headed for the kitchen.

"I'm not much of a wine drinker," he said. "But if you want, I can order a bottle."

Bella held up her glass. "This is fine for me. I may get one more, but then I'm done."

As they ate, the conversation revolved around their work and the Valley. When Bella asked about his life on Vancouver Island, Whip shrugged. "Not much to tell. Grew up there, went to tiny local schools through high school, then to Seattle for college."

"Oh?"

He smiled. "Don't look so surprised. I'm not a complete moron. I made it through all four years and even managed to graduate."

"I'm not surprised. I just pictured you as a cowboy from childhood. What was your major?"

"Environmental science."

"Now that fits."

"This trout is incredible. How's yours?"

"Delicious. Did your siblings follow your path?"

"My sister Addie majored in biology. She works for our dad now, and he's grooming her to take over when he retires."

"Not you?"

His eyes darkened, and Bella sensed he was fighting off emotions deeply buried. "Enough about me. I want to hear more about Big Sky Country. I love Montana. Almost moved there. Can't believe you and your brother moved down here. I mean, the Valley's amazing, but we're surrounded by desert and heat."

"Saguaro Valley is a great community. I came to be with Tom. He's in heaven here. He loves the stables, has great bosses, and look at the house they gave him. Are your bunkrooms nice?"

"State of the art, what else? I'll give you a tour sometime."

"I'd like that," she said, smiling at him.

WHIP INSISTED on paying even though she'd assumed they would split the bill. After saying good night to Edna and Nancy, they walked out into the night, the clear sky bursting with stars. As they strolled toward the car, Bella tripped on the gravel path and grabbed his arm. Instantly, he slipped his arm around her waist and held her close, a firm, steady grip that took her breath away.

"Thanks." She laughed nervously as she regained her balance. "This is why I seldom wear anything with heels."

"I'm glad you did," he said, lips close to her ear before he let her go.

The path that surrounded the property was, as usual, lit by thousands of twinkle lights. "Let's walk our dinner off, shall we?" she suggested, heading for the packed sandy walkway. Suddenly, feeling bold and reckless, she slipped out of her shoes and threw them to the side of the path. "Don't let me forget those, okay?"

Whip followed her, chuckling. "I'll try."

Walking backward, facing him, she said, "You know, my brother told me to stay off this path. Apparently, it's known as an after-dinner lover's lane."

"Is that so?" He marveled as the light played on her hair and lit up her beautiful eyes. *If she wasn't the boss's sister, I'd grab hold of her and kiss her silly, the little flirt.*

She paused until he caught up, then slipped her arm through his, resting her head on his shoulder. "Thanks for dinner. I'm not a big drinker, so I'm a little tipsy right now."

"Uh-huh." The warmth of her against him rocketed his libido into space.

"I like being tipsy, though."

Coming to his senses, he stopped. "I know what you're doing, Bella Jacobi."

"Oh, you do, do you? What's that?"

"Trying to get me fired."

"Whatever do you mean?"

She actually batted her eyelashes! "If you were anyone else, I'd haul you into the bushes and show you."

"Coward."

"Not a coward, just a realist. Come on, Ms. Tipsy. Time to get you home before Tom sends out the cavalry." He grabbed her shoes and opened the truck door, tossing them in.

Bella slid by him, her breasts brushing his arm, a smile on her face. As he closed the door she murmured, "Thanks."

CHAPTER 9

"Let's park up here and walk down," Bella said as they drove past the stables and the lot beside the bunkhouses. "That way, Mr. Nosey won't know we're home, and you can give me a tour of the bunkhouses."

Whip pulled in and killed engine. "Happy to walk you down, but touring the bunkhouses? Not a great idea."

"Why not? By the looks of things, no one's around."

"You're trouble."

"Come on, don't be a stick in the mud. Just a quick peek. I'll just see yours, then we'll be on our way."

He shook his head. "I'm gonna regret this, big-time. Come on, this way."

He unlocked the bunkhouse door on the unit nearest the stables and stepped aside. She swished by him into the open living area, a small kitchen—refrigerator, microwave, two-burner stove, and cabinet space—to one side. Bella wandered around, discovering the bedroom and bath down a short hallway. Everything, including the bedroom, was clean and orderly, bed made, clothes on peg racks lining one wall or hung in the large closet, light pine walls everywhere except the bathroom. The floors were pine boards, and in the living room area, large windows with attractive sage-green blinds looked out on acres of green fields and the training loops to the east. The bedroom windows faced the distant mountains.

"This is gorgeous. I bet your daytime view from here is amazing. Are they all like this?"

"Yup."

"If and when I move out of my brother's, I wonder if Ben and Spark would lease me one of these."

"Doubtful."

"Why?"

"You're not an employee of the stables, you're a woman, and they're all occupied."

"Maybe I could beg for a part-time job here and put my name on a bunkhouse list?"

"Good luck with that. Now come on, let's get you home."

"Party pooper," she said, strolling out the door, Whip on her heel, just as Greg's truck went past with several of the crew.

Catcalls and whistles pierced the still night. "Great," he muttered. *So much for keeping this under wraps.*

They walked side by side, not stopping to say hello to the men. Bella sensed his fury and felt guilty. She knew his job wasn't in danger, but he'd take a lot of grief before this blew over. Halfway to the farmhouse, she stopped, turning to face him. "I'm sorry. I shouldn't have imposed like that. It was juvenile and stupid." When she looked up, she was surprised to finding him grinning. "You're not mad?"

"There are worse things in life than being caught escorting a beautiful woman out of one's home. Be better if she wasn't the boss's sister, but hey, after the shit dies down, maybe I'll get some respect out of this."

"Oh?"

"Never mind. Let's get you in the house before something else happens." Hand on the small of her back, he nudged her onward.

His touch sent heat coursing through her from head to toe, and Bella's legs felt like limp noodles. *Almost there, girl,* she told herself, *almost there.*

People seldom locked their doors in the Valley, so Whip stepped forward and opened it for her.

Bella stepped inside and turned to him. "Well, good night, then."

"I better do this quick before your brother gets home," he said.

"Do what?"

In answer he drew her close and kissed her, lightly at first, then, as she responded, her arms circling his shoulders, his lips parted hers, and the kiss grew deeper. No telling where things would have gone if headlights hadn't crested the hill.

Instantly, he stepped back. "Tom."

"Yup," she said, reaching forward to squeeze his strong forearm. "Thanks for tonight. It was fun."

"Yeah, it was," he said, smiling. "Apology accepted, then?"

Bella laughed. "Of course, but to completely seal the deal, we might have to take another ride or have a lunch or two at Gracie's."

"Sounds good," he said, turning away as Tom appeared from the side yard.

"Hey, you two," he called. "Kind of late, isn't it?"

"Yeah, boss, gotta hit it. Early day tomorrow." Whip waved and headed up the hill, where he was soon swallowed by darkness.

Tom eyed his sister. "That was a quick getaway. Is there something I should know?"

Bella rolled her eyes as they stepped inside. "No. How was your night in Grenville?"

"Interesting. Good meal, but never saw the movie."

"Necking in the parking lot?"

"No, the projector broke."

"Bummer."

"Yeah it was, but we found things to do."

"I bet you did."

"So tell me about your friendly dinner."

"In the morning," she said, as she grabbed a glass of water and headed for the stairs. "I'm beat."

"Uh-huh. Night, sis."

CHAPTER 10

"So?" Tom said as Bella came into the kitchen. Dressed in jeans and a T-shirt, she was heading into town to have lunch with Gretchen Sullivan, one of her fellow midwives.

"So nothing. We had a great time, Vermillion's amazing, and that's all you need to know."

He frowned, running fingers through his thick, unruly hair. "Did you have to go to his bunkhouse? Jeez, Bella."

She threw up her hands, then went to grab her jacket and purse from the mudroom. "Oh my God, it's not even eight and you've already ferreted that out?"

"No ferreting involved. We're in the barn by five thirty, and your little rendezvous was the main topic of conversation. The guys were all giving Whip shit. How long were you in there?"

"Long enough to rip each other's clothes off and go at it, which we didn't."

"Ha-ha."

"This is ridiculous. Just suppose we actually began dating, which we won't, what would you do then? Forbid me to see him? Fire Whip?"

Tom shrugged, then shook his head, a smile on his face. "I don't know what I'd do. Nothing, except to warn him that if he broke your heart, I'd have to rip him to shreds."

"Please don't do that. Ever. I'm off. Having lunch with Gretchen from work, then doing a little shopping. You want anything in town or at the farms?"

"I can't think of anything. I'm making chili tonight, but I think we have everything."

"I'll pick up avocados and lettuce. See you."

On her drive into town, Bella thought about Whip and her brother's objections and wondered if there was something neither man was saying. Whip was definitely a mystery man, but did her brother know things about his past that he wasn't telling her? Or was he just concerned after Derek? There was also the question of how she felt about the handsome, enigmatic cowboy with whom she clearly shared a fiery attraction.

Whip met Nick Parker in the barn shortly after noon. "Hey, man," Nick said, "I was wondering if anyone was around."

"Just you and me. Remember, Bobby takes Sundays off. Let's see what the devil horse thinks of the two of us. Bobby's only here two more days, so he's gonna have to get used to us or it's bye-bye for him."

"Shame," Nick said as the two headed up to the round pen where Ghost stood alone, watchful.

"Yup, he's a beauty. The big bosses are stopping by this afternoon to take a look, so hopefully he'll be cooperative."

Nick gave him a raised eyebrow. "Got any horse tranquilizers?"

Predictably, Ghost spent most of the morning rearing and snorting at the two men. Just after lunch, Grace arrived to work with Dusty, which got him even more riled up. "Think we should move Grace and Dusty to the far corral?" Whip asked.

Nick nodded. "Probably best."

The two men worked for over an hour, Nick with the lead line,

Whip holding back, then trying to approach Ghost. Surprisingly, despite Nick's way with horses, Whip seemed to be less threatening to the stallion. Several times, he had managed to approach and actually touch Ghost's back. At such moments Nick let the lead go slack and Whip spoke softly with lots of "Hey, boys," as he neared the stallion.

Nick observed the two. "He knows you're not afraid, man. You're doin' great."

"Who the hell says I'm not afraid?" Whip whispered as voices came from the barn.

"Let's leave him be for a few minutes," Nick said. "He'll calm down."

"Let's hope so."

The two men walked to the edge of the pen to observe Grace and Dusty as she rode him around the pen.

"Hey, Grace, lookin' good," Nick said.

"Thanks," she said. "I've never ridden before, so Dusty and I are learning together."

Nick shook his head. "You'd never know it. Just goes to show that when horse and rider connect, everything falls into place."

Grace smiled. "Don't jinx us."

"Where's your fiancé today? Has he given up watching you two like a hawk?"

"Had to," Whip said, "or risk losing his job. They've been incredibly busy up there, and Harley depends on him. In addition to all his other talents, Tom's a much better schmoozer than Harley."

Nick laughed. "Tell me about it. It was hilarious watching Harley with Morgan's Run's snooty clients. He spends a lot of time biting his tongue." Before Ben and Spark hired him to run Valley Stables, Harley had spent years in charge of the Morgan's Run stables with Maggie, Jeb, and Nick. "Speaking of the good ole days, here come all four of the big bosses."

Whip turned to spy Tom and Harley headed up the rise from the barn, Ben, and Spark beside them. "We'd better say a few prayers and get back to Ghost."

"Hey, guys," Harley called as the group reached the round pen. "How's it going?"

"Ups and downs," Whip said, nodding to the others. Ghost immediately began pacing and snorting, clearly unsettled by the newcomers.

"He sure is a fine animal," Spark said.

After peering over at Grace and Dusty, Tom leaned against the fence. "We've made a little progress, but he's pretty unpredictable."

"No saddle, then?" Ben asked.

Whip chuckled. "That's a ways away, I'm guessing."

Nick picked up the twelve-foot training rope and held it loosely as Whip climbed into the ring. His eyes never left the stallion. "Hey, Whip, want to take over here? I think he's better with you."

Whip took the lead and turned to Ghost. "Hey, boy, good boy." He began a slow rhythmic twirling of the end of the training rope as he clucked, hupped, and made kissing sounds to encourage the horse to step back. Careful to stay at least three feet back so Ghost could see him and not get spooked, he moved closer.

Nick turned to the observers. "What he's doing is gently encouraging Ghost to retreat on command, rather than charging. As you know, horses have binocular vision, so they can't see when something or someone is in front of them within two feet or less."

Miraculously, the stallion began to step back, snorting, but complying. "Good boy," Whip said, taking the middle of the rope for shorter twirls at the horse's eye level. For a few minutes, Ghost remained calm, then suddenly, the rope came too close, and he reared, whinnying. His hooves lashed out. Whip stood his ground, reverting to wide twirls, but the stallion was clearly agitated and continued to rise up, bringing his body closer and closer to Whip.

"Try to tighten up a bit, control his head," Nick called, just as the stallion hit his mark and Whip crashed to the ground, struck in the shoulder by a black hoof. Nick grabbed the training whip and approached the stallion as Tom and Harley jumped the fence and dragged Whip out through the gate. As soon as the stallion retreated, Nick walked backward, taking his eyes off the horse only long enough to turn and jump the fence.

"I'll call for the ambulance," Tom said, as he pulled his cell phone from his pocket.

Grace left Dusty and ran down to meet them. "I can take him in my car."

"I'm fine, just a bump," Whip said, "And I'm sure as hell not goin' all the way to Grenville. He just grazed me. My fault. I pushed too hard."

Ben Morgan shook his head. "He's a magnificent horse, but this doesn't look promising. I'd like to talk to Bobby before he takes off. If he's not optimistic, we're gonna have find another place for Ghost. He's spooking the other horses and he's taking up too much time. The other horses are suffering, and we can't have him injuring his handlers."

Spark nodded. "I agree. Too much at stake."

Harley gazed over at Tom and Nick. "They're right, guys. Too much other work to do to spend all day with an aggressive, dangerous horse."

"Has Patty given him a thorough going-over to rule out any physical issues?" Ben asked.

"When he arrived, Patty looked him over as best she could, but thorough? That involves getting much closer than any of us dare," Tom said, watching Whip. "I think a doc should look at that shoulder."

"It's nothing," his assistant said as he brushed dust from jeans, then swung his arms in circles over his head. "See? I'll grab some ice and meds and I'll be fine."

"Okay, but I'm having Bella check you out when she gets home, and if she decides you need an X-ray, you're going. Deal?"

Whip nodded, gazing around at the group. "Sorry. I thought ole Ghost was gonna give you a good show." As he dropped his arm, he winced. *Gotta get that ice and heavy-duty ibuprofen ASAP!*

∼

GRETCHEN WAITED on the bench outside Gracie's Diner. When Bella arrived, her friend and colleague's eyes were closed, her head inclined upward. "Soaking in the sun?" Bella asked.

"Yes, and it feels heavenly," Gretchen said, standing to greet her, pale blue eyes warm. She had the thickest carrot-red hair Bella had ever seen, long and curly, tied back in a ponytail today. In jean capris and a white linen top, she looked lovely.

"Hey, gals," Gracie called, as they stepped into the diner. As usual, the place was packed.

"Sit wherever you can find a spot. We just put in two picnic tables on the back deck. Don't think anyone's out there. Just tell Maria if you go out so she'll find you."

Bella turned to her friend. "Deck?"

"Perfect."

They stopped to alert Maria, who was carrying a huge tray of food. "I'll be right out," she said. "Know what you want to drink?"

They both ordered iced coffees and headed for the back door.

"Great choice," Gretchen said as they sat down. "I never tire of looking at those gorgeous mountains."

"Me either. I feel really lucky. You're going to have to come out to the farmhouse for dinner with Tom and me. This is our view too."

"That place is supposed to be spectacular."

"It is. The long-held dream of two billionaires who have the means to make it happen."

"So you're glad you settled in the Valley," Gretchen said. "I mean it's beautiful, but pretty quiet, especially when we depend on Grenville for culture."

Bella laughed. "Tuscon's not a bad drive. Lots to do there."

"I 'spose," Gretchen replied, her voice wistful.

"Are you missing home?"

"Maybe a little. Mostly I've been lonely these past couple of years. Not all the time, though, and I was thrilled when you came on board."

"Have you dated at all since you moved here?" Bella asked as Maria set down their iced coffees.

"Have you ladies decided?" Maria asked, pad in hand.

"I'm going to have the loaded omelet with sweet potato hash-browns and no toast," Bella said, handing Maria the menu.

Gretchen looked up from her perusal. "So hard to decide. I think I'll have the same omelet, but with brussels sprouts hash and sour dough toast."

As Maria disappeared, Bella said, "Much healthier choice, the brussels sprouts."

"Sweet potatoes are very good for you. Now, back to my pathetic dating history. I've experimented with the whole online dating thing and had a few dinners and lunches. Nice guys, just no spark, you know? I also dated one of the docs at the hospital. Same thing. No spark."

"Bummer."

"How 'bout you?"

Bella rolled her eyes, brushing her hair from her forehead. "I came here shortly after a nasty breakup. I've been kind of lying low."

Gretchen smiled, eyeing her closely. "Oh? I could have sworn you've had the moony look of a new lover for the past week or so."

"Well, there is someone, actually. Someone with whom I'd never have imagined myself. I mean, he's a great guy and drop-dead gorgeous, but also kind of wild and wooly. Plus my brother is vehemently opposed to it."

"Why?"

"They work together. It's complicated."

They chatted a while about Whip, then moved on to other topics and their plans for next few months. Gretchen had just signed up for one of Robbie Morgan's adventure tours, a short three-night hiking trip in the western mountains, and she encouraged Bella to sign up. "Talk about gorgeous," she said, referring to Robbie. "Too bad he's engaged."

By the time Maria brought the check, Bella had forgotten all about Whip and the confusions surrounding him. They decided to do some shopping along Main Street and at Saguaro Dreams. Saguaro Dreams, or SD as it was known by Valley residents, was a three-story emporium of shops and art galleries specializing in local goods and art. Known throughout the Southwest, it was a draw for many looking for authentic local crafts, clothing, and artwork.

"Oh my goodness," Gretchen said as they meandered through one of SD's galleries. "There are some amazing paintings here, aren't there? Isn't that a Hope Seymour?"

"Looks like it," Bella said, stepping closer to a large landscape depicting the western mountains. "Oh, gosh, look at the price!"

"Yes, she gets top dollar. I would kill for one of her paintings, but I'd have to win the lottery to afford even a tiny one."

"There are some incredible works of hers at Morgan's Run and over at Spark Foster's castle," Bella said. "I don't know her well, but she seems like a lovely person. Did she grow up around here, do you know?"

"Tin Town, outside of Tucson. She came up to help her good friend Beth Morgan Langdon when her first child was born, and she and Robbie got together. As they say, the rest is history. She's in my yoga class, but they also live in my condo complex. That's how I know a little about her."

"She's an amazing artist, that's for sure," Bella said as she made a mental note to seek Hope out at the next social gathering.

As they were exiting SD, each with a couple of small purchases, Bella's phone rang. "What? When? I'll leave now. Be there in ten!" She clicked off and turned to Gretchen. "There's been an accident out at the stables. Whip's hurt. I've got to go."

"Of course. Would you like me to drive you?"

"No, I'm fine. This was lots of fun, Gretch. We'll do it again soon and also get you out to the farmhouse." She gave her a hug, then turned and ran the two blocks to her car.

CHAPTER 11

"Not his fault," Whip said as he and Tom observed the white stallion circling the corral. The bosses and Nick had departed. Occasionally, Ghost would come close to where they stood, calmer now, emitting soft snorts and nickers before he raced away. "See, he's trying to apologize."

"Maybe."

"It'd be shame to bring him this far, then give up."

"Can't say as we've brought him very far."

Whip winced as he moved his arm. "He doesn't have the wild look in his eyes anymore. Even when he was rearing, his eyes weren't crazy looking like when he first got here."

"More devious and calculating?"

"No, I pushed him too far too fast, and he was letting me know it."

"Well, prepare yourself, 'cause if the bosses decide he goes, he goes. Great, Bella's home," Tom said as he turned to spy her SUV coming down the hill.

"Yippee, someone else to fuss over me."

"It's either that or off to Grenville Hospital."

"Fine."

The two men walked back down to the barn, meeting Bella just outside the door. "How are you?" she asked.

"A little sore, but fine," Whip said, his body temperature already rising at the prospect of her touch.

She smiled. "Can I take a look?"

"Your brother says it's that or off to Grenville."

She waved toward a bench at the side of the barn. "Why don't you sit and take off your shirt?"

As Tom and Bella watched, he pulled his dusty T-shirt over his head. Bella gasped at the sight of his muscular tan body. Both men stared at her, and she said, "A bit of dust caught in my throat."

Tom frowned. "Dust, huh?"

Whip grinned and sat down.

After a deep breath, Bella swallowed and came to stand beside him. "Can you raise your arms over your head?" He did and began swinging them around. "Okay, that's enough." As he lowered them, she noticed he winced. A welt was already rising on his right shoulder.

Gently, she took hold of his right hand and upper arm and manipulated them. "How does that feel?"

He winced as she moved the arm upward. "Okay."

She gave him the eye. "You don't look like it feels okay, but I don't think anything's broken."

"I know there's nothing broken."

"Let's get ice on that now. Is there any in the barn fridge?"

"I'll grab one of the ice packs we use for the horses," Tom said and disappeared into the barn.

"Get a bottle of water too!" Bella called. She realized she still held his forearm and let go. She reached into her bag and pulled out a bottle of ibuprofen. "I'm going to suggest that you take four of these now and four tonight."

"Thanks."

"You can get something stronger. A really high dosage of this, but I can't prescribe it because I'm not your doctor."

"This'll be fine. I'm tough." He looked up and grinned.

She loved his smile, even his teasing one, but she refused to get lost in those gray eyes. "Once the shock wears off, it may be tricky using that arm till the swelling goes down."

"Lucky I'm left-handed, then."

"Yes." She could hear her brother talking on the phone inside as she stared down at Whip. "So, what happened?" He gave her a quick recap of the incident, after which she said, "Too bad. He's such a beautiful horse."

"I haven't given up on him yet, and they shouldn't either. The bosses have given us till Tuesday."

Bella smiled. "Fingers crossed."

They could hear Tom finishing his call inside.

"Have lunch or dinner with me this week."

"What?"

"Just say yes. I'll call you later and work out the details."

"Yes," she heard herself reply as her brother appeared with an ice pack and water.

Bella handed Whip the water and pills, then gently helped him put on his shirt.

Tom observed, his gaze appraising the situation. "You don't look too comfortable, buddy. Why don't you take that ice pack up to the bunkhouse and lie down?"

"I can drive you," she said.

"Thanks, but I'm not dead yet."

Much as he didn't want to throw them together, Tom said, "Don't be an ass. Take the damn ride and go to bed. Greg and the guys can take care of things down here."

"Maybe an hour or two, but I'll be down to help bring the horses in," Whip said as he followed her to the car.

"We'll see," his boss said, shaking his head as he watched the two.

Several minutes later, Bella pulled her SUV alongside the bunkhouses and looked over at her passenger. "Need help with anything before I go?"

He hopped out and swung his arms around. "Do I look like I need help?"

She noticed he was gritting his teeth. "All right, Superman, just keep icing. Fifteen minutes on, half hour off, then repeat."

"Yes, ma'am," he said, tipping his hat. "How's Tuesday night?"

"Excuse me?"

"Dinner?"

"Okay, that'd be great."

"Gracie's or Bulldog? Or would you rather go fancy?"

"I vote Bulldog."

"Pick you up at seven?"

"Only if you're feeling up to it."

"Oh, I'll be up to it, no worries there." Another tip of the hat.

"Okay, cowboy. Now go in there and rest."

She watched him stroll up to his unit and then pulled away.

CHAPTER 12

During Monday's and Tuesday's training sessions, things went from bad to worse with Ghost continually confronting Bobby and refusing to back down. No one was injured, but no one dared go near him either. "He's a great horse, but this is gonna take months, maybe years," Bobby said on Tuesday. He, Whip, and Greg were eating lunch in the shade of the barn. "I can't lie to your bosses. If they're willing to hang in with him, you never know what you'll accomplish, but I'm obligated somewhere else for the next month. I could come back in about six weeks, though not for long."

Whip shrugged, tossing a sandwich wrapper in the trash. "Maybe he'll be on his best behavior this afternoon when Ben and Spark come. Unfortunately, he gets really rattled by visitors, and there have been a lot of human and wildlife visitors lately."

"Oh yeah?"

"Coyotes have been around a lot. Morgan's Run has lost a few lambs and calves and

We hear them howling behind the bunkhouses every night."

"Mating season," Bobby said. "Thanks for the grub. My sister says there've been a few cougar sightings too."

"Hikers have seen 'em," Whip said, standing abruptly. "I've got a couple of things to take care of in the barn, and I'll meet you out there."

"Uh-oh, touched a nerve," the horse whisperer said, turning to Greg, his gaze full of questions. "Had an incident with a mountain lion, has he?"

Greg shrugged. "If he has, he never talks about it. Whip doesn't talk much about himself or his past."

"You're never the same once you've stared into those greenish-yellow cougar eyes. Dead eyes. Killer eyes."

Greg stared at him. "Sounds like you have?"

"Once, on the trail. Fortunately, my shotgun was handy."

"Did you kill it, then?"

"Naw, just fired a warning shot and it disappeared. It had been stalking me for half the day, so I was prepared."

"Can a mountain lion kill a horse?"

"Sure can. In many wild areas, mustangs are the cougars' main diet. Mothers teach their young ones to hunt them."

"So, you're saying keep your gun handy if you're out on the trail, then?"

"Depends. I understand you usually don't see many cougars around here, so it may be a freak year. Maybe their food supply dwindled and they're comin' lower. You gotta hope they don't stay long. Hate to kill 'em, but once they start hunting domestic animals or people, you don't have a choice. Pepper spray doesn't hold them off for long or prevent killing." He threw his empty soda can in the recycle bin. "Guess I'd better get to it."

When Bobby got to the round pen, Ghost was circling Whip, who held the training lead loosely in his left hand. As the trainer hopped over the fence, he said, "Maybe not the best move given the morning we've had."

"Tryin' to get him a little further along before they get here."

"Okay, let's try something different. We're gonna actually use the whip, just a few times till he gets the idea that we're in charge," Bobby said. He took the training stick from Whip and attached a line to the end. He then ran at Ghost, pointing first, then calling and shouting,

"Ya, ya," smacking his butt to get him moving. The horse pinned back his ears, but then followed Bobby's lead around and around the pen. Finally, the trainer turned and walked toward the fence. The stallion stood still and watched him, almost docile.

Whip let out a low whistle. "Wow."

Bobby handed him the stick. "Your turn, and don't be a wimp."

The second the training stick changed hands, Ghost reared, snorted, and pinned his ears back, ready to charge. "Okay, now," Bobby said, "Lunge and go after him, show him who's boss."

While not as confident and forceful, particularly with his sore arm, Whip moved forward and mimicked the trainer. Miraculously, Ghost responded and began circling the pen. Whip continued to lunge at him, pointing and yelling. This went on for five minutes until Bobby called, "Give him a breather. Yourself too. Turn and walk away."

Both men turned just as Ben, Spark, and Tom appeared. The minute their backs were turned, with a shriek and a snort, Ghost ran right at them.

"Watch out," Tom cried as the two men cleared the fence just in time. When they looked back, Ghost reared up, triumphant, crashing his hooves against the fence.

Ben shook his head. "Guess we have our answer. A shame. Thoughts Bobby?"

"We turned our backs too soon, but we've made progress today. Whip knows what he has to do, and I'll leave some videos that may be helpful. You could consider gelding him."

Ben shook his head. "It can take six months to a year for a horse to calm down after gelding. Whip has a full day of work every day that does not include hours working with a killer horse." He looked over at Spark, who nodded in agreement. "Next thing you know, he seriously injures someone or one of the other horses. I'm sorry, son. He's just too dangerous. It's too much of a risk. Spark, Tom, Harley, and I all agree, he has to go. We'll start looking into options tomorrow."

Whip gazed at the stallion now standing at the far end of the pen, pawing the ground. "Sorry, boy," he said, handing the training stick to Bobby. "I've got chores. Excuse me." With that, he strode off toward the barn.

"Damn shame, but we have no choice," Spark said, looking at Tom.

"He'll get over it," Tom said. "I'll make some calls in the morning. See if I get any leads on placements."

As they headed toward the drive and Spark's enormous SUV, they all knew what Ghost's fate was likely to be. Many of the dealers buying wild horses now, no matter what they claimed, eventually shipped them to Mexico or overseas for slaughter.

As the bosses drove away, Tom found Whip in Dusty's stall, the Kiger standing still and quiet for a brushing. When he spied his boss, Whip raised a hand. "I don't want to talk about it."

"Fine. They're right, you know. The liability on a horse like that is huge."

"That's talkin' about it," Whip snapped, a very uncharacteristic response to his boss. While they were friendly, the two men were not exactly friends, and they had thus far maintained a respectful, professional relationship.

"I've got to head up to the stables. Be back in an hour or two to help with feeding. After today, don't attempt to bring Ghost in or out of the barn by yourself."

"Whatever."

"I'm serious, Kittredge."

Whip shrugged, but made no further remark.

CHAPTER 13

"Dinner?" Tom asked, gazing at his sister. "What the hell is that about?"

"Two friends having dinner," she said, moving about the kitchen, packing her lunch for tomorrow's workday.

"Not great timing. He's in rough shape."

"Why?"

"Bosses lowered the boom on Ghost. He's going as soon as they can make arrangements."

"Whip's attached to Ghost, isn't he?"

"Seems like it. The guy's a loose cannon right now. Maybe you should call it off, go next week."

"Don't be ridiculous. Isn't Grace coming out for dinner."

"Yup."

"Well then, there you go."

"What are you talkin' about?"

"Privacy? You'll have the house to yourselves. You can have a nice intimate dinner for two with your fiancée?"

He raised an eyebrow. "We'd be happy to have you join us."

And cook the dinner, she thought. "Well, I'm going to the Bulldog with Whip, so too bad. Now I've gotta take a shower."

After showering and dressing in jeans and a soft blue top, its vee neck revealing a hint of cleavage, Bella headed downstairs. She could hear Tom and Grace talking in the kitchen and popped her head in. "Hi, you two."

"Wow, you look sensational, Bella," Grace said.

"She's not supposed to look sensational."

Grace gave her fiancé a quizzical look.

"Ignore him," Bella said, grabbing her purse. "What're you guys making for dinner anyway?"

Tom had his head in the fridge, rummaging around. "Not sure yet. We're gonna see what we have."

"Uh-huh," Bella said, wondering as she always did how her brother hadn't died of starvation or excessive takeout food before her arrival. Grace wasn't much better. Whenever the three of them ate together, Bella prepared the meal. *Hopeless*, she thought as she spied dust in the drive. "That's my ride. Have a great dinner!" she said, heading for the front door.

"No big brother glowering from the porch tonight?" Whip asked as she slipped into the truck.

"No. Thank God, Grace is there. He behaves better when she's around. They're currently searching through the fridge and cabinets for dinner fixings. Two of the most clueless people when it comes to cooking."

"Me too." He drove past the stables and onto the property's long drive. "I mean, I can cook, but why bother here? Fran, our cook, is fantastic."

"I have got to get into one of those bunkhouses!" she said. "I love Fran's cooking."

She referred to Frances Barstock, who Ben and Spark had hired just a few weeks back. Before that, the crew had been either fixing their own meals or eating mountains of takeout, especially pizza.

"Maybe you can bunk with Fran. She's in one of the apartments above the stables.

"Hmm... Who's in the other?"

"Patty."

"Hmm...yes, Patty. Not one of my favorite people," Bella said.

He looked over in surprise. "What's the matter with her?"

"I don't know... She's never been very friendly, I guess. Truth be told, I haven't made much of an effort either."

Whip grinned. "Patty's okay. Maybe a bit uptight. She's a good vet. I only wish she could've gotten a better look at Ghost just to make sure his aggression isn't related to pain or some kind of illness."

Bella stared at him. "Do you think it might be?"

He shrugged. "Dunno." He pulled into a parking spot on Main Street several blocks from the Bulldog.

Bella hopped out before he could open her door. "I forgot to do this when I saw you," she said. She draped arms round his shoulders and kissed him. Whip responded, pulling her closer. "Whoa, cowboy, not on Main Street," she said, stepping back, breathless.

"You started it," he said as he let her go.

"It was meant to be a hello kiss, not a drag-me-off-in-the-bushes kiss," she said, smiling as she turned and headed for the Bulldog.

"Hello kiss, huh?"

"Yup, it's my new thing."

Is your new thing also waving your perfect ass at me? he thought, shaking his head. Whip wanted her more than he'd ever wanted any woman, but this was playing with fire and his job.

CHAPTER 14

The Bulldog was surprisingly busy for a Tuesday night. The darts league played in the crowded back room, the bar was full, and most of the booths were occupied. "There's one empty booth halfway down," Whip said, pointing. "You go grab it, and I'll get drinks. What would you like?"

"Desert Amber," she said.

"Really?" he asked, but she'd already turned and was sashaying toward the empty booth.

Bella waved over her shoulder. "When in Rome!"

What the hell's happened to her? he thought, wondering if she'd fallen off a horse and hit her head. He turned to the owner. "Hey, Russ, two Desert Ambers. On second thought, I'll take a pitcher and two glasses."

"Comin' right up. You go ahead. I'll have Jackie bring 'em down and clean off the table."

"Thanks, man."

When Whip got to the table, Bella was chatting with Jackie, who was already wiping the table. "Hey, Jackie," he said. "How's tricks?"

"Hoppin'. I'll be lucky if I don't get a dart in my ass with those yahoos. They're especially obnoxious tonight."

"Give a holler if you need backup," he said. "I just ordered a pitcher of Desert Amber from Russ."

"Okay, hon, be right back."

As Jackie departed, Bella said, "Another Whip Kittredge admirer, I see."

"Ha-ha. So, what's up with you tonight? You seem... I don't know, you just seem different. Flirty, I guess."

"I can be flirty."

"I believe you."

"There's a lot about me you don't know," she said, leaning across the table, her glorious breasts on display thanks to her vee-neck.

Whip leaned back, folding arms across his chest. "Is that so?"

Suddenly, she burst out laughing. "You're right, of course."

"About?"

"Me. This isn't me, flirting like some kind of babe."

He grinned. "You are some kind of babe."

"Very funny. I don't know how to flirt."

"You were doin' a pretty good job of it. You certainly had my attention. Couldn't wait to see what you were gonna do next."

Jackie interrupted, setting down the pitcher of beer and two iced mugs. "You guys know what you want?"

"Bella?" he asked.

She gazed up at the waitress. "Bulldog burger, sauce on the side and a green salad instead of fries. Thanks."

"What about you, hon?" Buxom and curvaceous, Jackie leaned in, brushing strands of her dark hair from her forehead.

"Straight Bulldog burger, curly fries, and extra sauce. Thanks, Jack."

Straightening, she pulled herself together with a "Be back soon" and disappeared.

"So?" he said.

"So what?"

"Were you gonna tell me something about your sudden urge to flirt?"

"I guess I'm just tired of playing by the rules, playing it safe, letting men pursue me, listening to my big brother, everything. I'm thirty-two years old! Tom has no right to say anything about who I date. It's ridiculous. And you're off somewhere I can't reach, like a door slammed in my face. I'm not blaming you. I'm just frustrated! I like you. I'm attracted to you, big-time, and for some reason, that's a bad thing." She paused, meeting his eyes. "I guess that about sums up my present state."

"Wow."

"Wow? That's all you have to say?"

"I'm not sure what to say. Not sure what you want me to say."

"Well, to start, you could say how you feel, or maybe try to characterize your state."

He scratched his forehead, then smiled. "Not sure men are great at characterizing our states, as you put it, or at least I'm not. I won't lie. There's some shit in my past that gets in the way sometimes. Pops up when I least expect it. Kind of out of the blue. I shut down when it happens. Survival, I guess."

"I'm sorry."

"Don't be. It's my problem. But as far as the rest...about you. Well, the thing is, I'm crazy about you, but I like it here and like my job. This is the first place that's felt like home since I left the island. Not sure how something between us might go over with the bosses, a certain one in particular."

"Well, that one I can handle, and what little I know about the big bosses and Harley, I doubt any of them would give a shit. In fact, they'd probably be happy for us. They're the least snooty people I know. I mean Leonora Morgan, maybe, but even she comes around. According to what I've heard, the snootiness is all show for her Cowgirls, but in real life, she's pretty down to earth."

"Oh jeez, I hadn't even thought about her," he said, nodding as Jackie set down their food.

"Can I get you anything else?" Jackie asked.

"Thanks, all set," he said, and she hurried off.

Bella smiled, reaching across the table to take his hand. "Did I hear you say you were crazy about me?"

He wrapped his fingers around hers. "Yeah, but there's also the part about me being crazy and messed up too."

"We have a start, though, don't we?" she said softly.

"Yeah, I guess we do," he replied, gray eyes warm and gentle.

They ate chatting about day-to-day topics. Bella couldn't finish her burger and asked Jackie for a to-go box. Whip had no trouble finishing his meal, right down to the last curly fry.

CHAPTER 15

As Whip slowed the truck and turned into Valley Stables, Bella said, "I've got an idea. Why don't I grab my medical bag out of my car, and we could go down to the stables? Maybe Ghost will be calmer at night, and I could take a look at him."

"I'm not sure that's a good idea. Too dangerous."

"Not if you hold him and keep him calm."

"Yeah, right."

Whip pulled to a stop near the farmhouse, and she jumped out and ran to her car, praying her brother wouldn't notice they'd returned. Grace's SUV was in the drive, so Bella hoped he'd be occupied with more interesting pursuits. "Got it!" she said, sliding back into the truck.

Whip drove on and pulled up at the far side of the barn. As she moved to open her door, he reached over and held her back. "Okay, here's the deal, and you have to promise before we go in. First sight of distress, you back off."

"Absolutely."

"I mean it, Bella. Yes, I've grown attached to him, but he's still a really dangerous animal who could kill one or both of us if we spook him."

"I promise," she said, her voice grave. "Now, come on."

Shrouded in shadow, they entered the quiet barn, the silence punctuated by the occasional snort or nicker. Whip switched on the lights. Most horses were sleeping, but a few curious noses appeared as they made their way to the opposite end where Ghost's stall was separated from the others. When they peeked in, he too appeared to be sleeping.

"Do you think he'll mind if we wake him?" she whispered.

"Guess we're gonna find out," Whip replied, as he grabbed a halter and lead and a handful of oats from a nearby bucket. After shoving the oats in his pocket, he opened the door and slipped into the stall. "Hey, boy, hey, boy."

Ghost stirred and came forward, allowing Whip to rub his nose for a very brief time and fasten the halter over his head. "Hey, boy, good boy," he said. "This is new. He's let me do this a few times, but not for long."

Once Ghost was haltered, Bella came in with her stethoscope out and whispered, "Can you bring him broadside so I can try to take a listen?"

He reached into his pocket, retrieving the oats, which he offered to the stallion. Ghost nickered and snuffled them up as Bella listened to his chest.

"Not sure what I'm looking for, but his lungs are clear and his heart sounds strong. I'll look up a few things when I get back to my computer. What about his mouth? Think we could take a peek?"

"Not hopeful, but we can give it a try. Whatever you're planning to do, be ready, because we'll probably only have a second or two before he bites me."

The light was dim, so Bella grabbed her otoscope. "I'm pretty sure vets use a speculum to examine horses' mouths, but I don't have an equine speculum, and I doubt he'd let us use it anyway. Maybe if you feed him a few oats to distract him, I could lift his lips and at least peek at his gums."

"Okay, but if he bites one of us, don't be surprised." Whip scooped up a handful of oats from the cup and offered them to the stallion as Bella gently lifted the right side of Ghost's lip.

"Ouch," she said as she shined the otoscope along his gum line. "His mouth is loaded with blisters, poor thing. These must be really painful."

Suddenly, Ghost shook his head, shrugging her fingers from his lips and knocking the otoscope to the floor. The instrument fell inside the stall, and before one of them could retrieve it, the stallion struck out, black hoof smashing it to bits.

"The big stinker," Whip said. "He knew exactly what he was doing too."

"Poor guy," she said. "We should get the broken pieces out of there in case he tries to eat them."

While Whip held Ghost's lead at the rear of the stall, Bella quickly picked up the broken pieces of her otoscope and stepped out again. As the door closed behind her, he slipped off Ghost's halter and followed her. "Okay, boy, we'll let you get to sleep," he said softly, watching as Ghost began pacing.

"He must be having trouble eating with all those open sores. You need to get Patty in here to assess him. It looked like he also has a couple of jagged sharp teeth on his right side. They cause irritation and should probably be floated to smooth the edges. I had a horse they had to do that floating to all the time. As for the blisters, it looks topical. Like something he's eaten."

"I'll tell your brother, even though he'll probably bite my head off for letting you get near him. He can get Patty down here. You think this might be affecting his behavior?"

"Yes, I do, although he is a wild horse."

"Call it a night?" he asked, as Bella closed her medical bag. His eyes were glued to her sweet round ass as she bent to her task.

"Guess so," she said, as they walked side by side to the barn door. Their arms brushed against one another several times in gestures that were not completely random.

At the door, he switched off the lights and turned to her in the dark. "Thanks for doing that. Not sure it'll help poor ole Ghost if they're determined to ship him off, but maybe it'll buy him some time."

"My pleasure," she said. She reached up and touched his cheek. "I love horses and hate to see them suffer."

"Me too," he said, his voice gruff as they moved closer. "This is probably a bad idea."

Bella circled her arms around his neck. "I love bad ideas."

"Are you sure?" he asked, hands on her waist, his body in flames at her touch.

"What do you think, cowboy?"

"I think you've lost your mind, but I want you like I've never wanted a woman before. Come on." He took her hand and led her to the hay loft ladder. "Probably safer up there in case your brother sees the truck and comes tearing down here."

Bella started climbing, Whip one step below her, one hand on her ass. "I can do it myself, you know."

"Yeah, but this is more fun."

They reached the hayloft and tumbled into a pile of soft hay.

"Why isn't this pile baled like the rest?" she asked.

"This is the fallout. We clear it out every few weeks."

"Lucky me that you're behind in your housekeeping."

He could see her smile in the moonlight streaming through the window. Her smile and those beautiful caramel eyes. "Yeah, lucky you." He drew her close, lips capturing hers in a deep kiss, expressing a longing he'd carried his whole life.

Startled by his sudden ardor, Bella gave herself to him in a way she never had with Derek or any man. Her tongue teased and stroked his as she ran her fingers through his long, thick hair. When he moved his hand to her breast, she gasped as sensations streaked through her. For a rough and tumble cowboy, his touch was surprisingly gentle as his fingers slipped beneath her top to her back, unhooking her bra.

"You've done this before," she whispered, her breath catching in her throat as he took her breast into his hands, teasing and stroking the nipples to excruciating nubs of sensation.

"Beginner's luck," he said, trailing kisses down her neck, then taking one breast, then the other into his mouth as Bella writhed to orgasm.

She felt his erection pressed against her belly and began a rhythmic dance with her hips against his hardness, pleased that he now appeared to be breathless. There was something almost primal about this man, wild and untamed. As he deftly slipped off her jeans and panties, she wondered if he was a wizard and she'd fallen under his spell. Her last rational thought as his fingers opened her legs and slipped into her was *take me, take me, wherever you're going, take me with you!*

Not sure if she'd spoken aloud, there was no need. He'd thrown off his jeans and was suddenly inside her, deep inside her, thrusting gently at first, then, as she responded, lifting her hips to meet him. He drove deeper as they moved in unison, a kind of hungry, frenzied rutting that rocketed them to a crashing simultaneous climax. As the waves of ecstasy rode over them, their bodies slowly stilled, and he brought her closer.

"Jeez," he whispered, nibbling, then kissing her earlobes and neck.

"I have to agree with you," she said, kissing his chest, wondering if she'd made the biggest mistake of her life or the smartest one.

They lay in each other's arms, the moonlight streaming in, and fell asleep. Sounds from below startled them awake. "Bella! Whip! Where the hell are you," Tom called.

"Shit," Whip whispered.

"If we don't make a sound, maybe he'll go away," she said. *No such luck.*

"If you're up in that hayloft, you'd better come down, or you'll scare the horses."

This is ridiculous, Bella thought, moving away from Whip's warmth and sitting up. "Go back to the house, Tom! We're fine, and I'll be home soon."

Without a word, they listened as her bother stomped out of the barn. Whip crawled to the window and peered out. Sure enough, his boss was stalking up the hill to the farmhouse. His body language told it all. "Guess I'll be lookin' for work tomorrow," he muttered, scooting back to sit beside her, searching for his clothes.

"Don't be absurd!"

He pulled her into his arms. "It was worth it, though."

"Really?"

"Really." He kissed her lightly on the forehead. "Now let's get dressed and get you home before the boss sounds the alarm."

Fully dressed, they climbed down the loft ladder and went to check on Ghost. He was calm and half asleep, so arm in arm, they exited, trying not to make a sound. When they stepped out into the night, he said, "Guess I didn't hide the truck well enough."

"He probably saw the barn lights," she said, leaning into him as the strolled to the truck.

"Don't worry about him. I'll take care of things in the morning. He's acting like a Neanderthal, and it's got to stop."

"He's protecting you with good reason."

She gazed up at him. "What's that supposed to mean?"

"Nothing. Forget it. Let's go." He headed for the driver's side of the truck.

Puzzled, Bella opened her door and hopped in. "Are you okay?"

"Fine. Just late." He started the truck and drove the short distance up the hill. When he stopped, he turned to her. "You okay to go in by yourself?"

"Of course," she said, grabbing hold of her bag. "Whip, what's wrong?"

"Nothing. Out you go," he said, forcing a smile.

Once again, he had shut down, going to an unreachable place where she was unwelcome. "Okay, well, night, then." She leaned over, intending to kiss him, but he pulled back and touched her cheek.

"Night, Bella," he said, voice husky.

She sat still and silent for a minute, watching him stare straight ahead. "Okay, then... Night," she said, sliding out and shutting the door. As soon as she rounded the truck, he gunned the engine and drove away.

Hurt and confused, she headed up the front walk. Tom was seated on the sofa in the semidarkness. She raised her hand. "Not a word. I'm going to bed, and we'll talk about this in the morning." With that, she stomped up the stairs and slammed the door to her room.

Men, she thought as she stood in the bathtub, hot water cascading over her. *I'll never understand them as long as I live, and they clearly don't understand women!*

CHAPTER 16

"All I'm asking is that you cool it for a week or two. Is that so difficult?" Tom asked as he watched his sister preparing her lunch for work.

"Not difficult, just stupid." They'd been arguing about her relationship with Whip for twenty minutes, and she felt a headache coming on.

"Okay, so it's stupid, arbitrary, and idiotic. Fine. But would you indulge your big brother for once?"

"Why?"

"Because there's been a lot going on. A little time apart will give you both a chance to process the whole thing."

"Process? That's the most ridiculous word, especially for this situation."

"Bella, please." He grabbed her hand as she finished wrapping her tuna fish sandwich in waxed paper. I'm going to make the same request of him."

"What are we? Kindergarteners?"

"You're people I care about."

Bella gazed into his brown eyes and saw genuine concern and love shining back at her. She let out a deep sigh. "Okay, fine. We'll cool it. Hello and goodbye, period."

"Thank you."

She stuffed her lunch into her backpack and threw the pack over her shoulder. "That is unless we can't control ourselves and I rip his clothes off the minute I see him."

"Very funny."

"Have a good day. I hope you can get Patty down to look at Ghost's mouth. It's a mess."

"Will do. Thanks for checking him over. The stables will pay for a new otoscope, by the way."

"Great."

Tom shook his head. "We should have tried harder sooner."

"Think it'll change Ben's and Spark's minds about keeping him?"

Tom shrugged. "We can drag our heels a bit finding a placement and see how he does with treatment, but they seem pretty determined. They've got a lot on their minds and don't want to be dealing with an aggressive horse right now."

"Fingers crossed. Bye," she said as she headed out.

MIDWAY THROUGH THE MORNING, the crew was cleaning out stalls and Tom caught Whip as he headed up to check on Ghost.

After Tom made the same request he'd made to Bella, Whip said, "I hear you, man. I wish I could say I'm great relationship material, but I'd be lying."

"Don't sell yourself short, buddy. I'm not, but my sister went through hell with her loser, asshole boyfriend, and she's just getting her balance back."

"I understand. You have my word."

"Thanks," Tom said, extending his hand, which Whip grasped in a firm handshake.

"On a different subject, my folks are coming into town in a couple of weeks. Did I tell you that?"

"Yeah, when?"

"They're arriving week after next."

"Where're they staying?"

"The Morgan's Run Lodge."

"Fancy."

"Yeah, my mom loves it there. I think you were out of town on their last visit. Aside from saying hello to me, they're coming so Dad can talk with Robbie Morgan about their similar businesses. He wants to pick his brain. I wouldn't be surprised if he's considering turning the company over to my sister, Addie. She's coming too."

"Great, I look forward to meeting them. We can have a dinner here at the house, if you like, and I'm sure the Morgans will wine and dine you."

"I'm not much good at wine-and-dine things."

Tom laughed. "Neither am I. Listen, I've gotta head up to the stables. You got everything under control down here?"

"No prob."

"Be careful with the stallion. I'll ask Patty to come down as soon as she's free."

"Thanks, boss."

As Whip watched the tall cowboy head up the hill, he wondered whether things could get any stranger. *Maybe I'll check and see if that shrink in town has time for me*, he thought as he neared Ghost's corral.

The stallion stood at the fence as if waiting for him. Not his usual behavior. Ghost was usually pacing at the far end of the pen or snorting in the direction of the other horses, his huffing and puffing most often directed at Dusty.

"Hey, boy," Whip said, reaching over the fence to give him a gentle pat. The horse shook his head slightly, but didn't seem to mind. "Are you gonna be a good boy today? I have a ton of work to do, but I'll be back later, and we'll get down to it, okay?" Ghost snorted in reply before trotting off.

Whip walked down to the barn to find Greg and two of the other wranglers, Warren and Ramon, who were halfway through the stall mucking. "Hey, guys. I've gotta head up to the stables for an hour or so, then I'll be back to help with the fencing. Tom thinks we should get the leaf blowers out before you lay the fresh hay."

Greg pushed his hat back, gazing at his boss in surprise. "Really? I thought that was only for up top?"

Whip smiled. Greg was a hard worker, but he loved to question anything new, anything that diverged from the usual routines. "Apparently, they're running tours during next weekend's exhibition. Some of the high rollers expressed interest in seeing the rescue operation down here."

"So shouldn't we wait till Friday or Saturday to get the blowers out?"

Whip raised an eyebrow. "This is a trial run. Ben and Spark are coming by with Harley to look over the barn and yards, discuss things we can do to spruce up the place."

"Lucky us."

"I dare you to find a stable that pays you as much as here. Not to mention one with our living quarters and meals."

"I know, I know. Can you throw a couple of the blowers in your truck when you come back, boss?" Warren asked. "There's only one down here. They're around the side of the stables where we left 'em earlier. They need cleaning, but we can do that, then do these stalls."

"Will do," Whip said, leaving them to their work.

When he arrived at the stables, he spied Tom talking to Harley and Patty.

"Kittredge," Harley called. Using his last name was never a good sign.

"Yeah, boss?"

"You and Bella took a stupid risk fooling around with that stallion last night."

"He's getting gentler every day," Whip said, gazing from one to the other of them.

Harley frowned. "Not gentle enough to be sticking a hand in his mouth."

"Sorry I didn't check first. We were real careful."

"No more crazy shit, though, comprende?"

Whip nodded.

Patty looked over at him. "I'm swamped this morning, but I'll come down sometime after lunch. Will you be around?"

"Yeah, thanks. I'm repairing fences most of the day, so if you don't see me, ask one of the guys to call me."

"Speaking of fences," Harley said, "not that a fence will matter, but two farmers have seen cougars. They've killed a bunch of sheep at Morgan's Run. All of us need to be extra careful. For some reason, they're coming down lower right now. My brother-in-law's company has had to revise one of his adventure tours and Morgan's Run has canceled longer pack trips until the rangers can get a better sense of what we're dealing with.

Harley paused, staring at Whip. "You okay? You've gone as white as your stallion."

"Fine. I'm fine. Slight headache, that's all."

"Well, vigilance is the name of the game, guys. We've got million-dollar racehorses up here, and we can't afford a mountain lion right now. I've hired a couple of marksmen for the night shift."

CHAPTER 17

The Valley and its surrounding areas were experiencing a mini baby boom, and the midwives from Bella's practice worked practically around the clock, often with two of them at a delivery. For several weeks, Bella barely saw her brother, never mind Whip and the rest of the crew. She missed Scrabble Night and chorus and collapsed into bed each night exhausted. Weeks passed until one Tuesday, she and Tom shared a meal together, a late supper of grilled trout, a summer salad, and smashed potatoes. The potatoes were their mother's recipe.

"Thanks for cooking, Belle. Delicious. Mom would be proud."

She gave him a tired smile. "Now that she's living on Lean Cuisine and takeout."

He shrugged. "Who knows what those two eat down in Florida. With all their newfound wealth, they probably have a full-time chef." Their parents had made many millions selling their Montana properties, enabling them to live very comfortably in Naples. Neither of their offspring had seen their new home, but reports from friends and their relatives who'd visited and the real estate photos their mom sent at the time of the purchase were of a spectacular property near the water.

"So, what's new?" she asked. "I feel like I haven't seen you in years."

"Not much. Everyone's on high alert because of the mountain lion sightings. Lots of warnings up for riders and hikers. Pain in the neck."

"Ruthie told me you've had to post guards at the stables."

"Yup. They're getting really sophisticated surveillance cameras and equipment installed, but until they do, they're keeping the guards. My guess is they'll keep at least one person to monitor the cameras once they're up and running."

"I haven't seen the crew much. How are they doing?" she asked, gazing up, but not meeting his eyes.

"Same ole same ole."

"Oh?"

"Seem fine to me. You asking about anyone in particular?"

"You know I am since I've...we've been abiding by your idiotic request not to see each other."

"No calls, no nothing?"

"The truth? I've tried him a couple of times, but it always goes to voicemail. He hasn't called me, so you can give him a gold star."

"To answer your question, he seems okay. His folks arrive tomorrow, so he's been busy with that."

"Oh? Where are they staying?"

"Lodge over at Morgan's Run. Apparently, they've stayed there once before. His dad's coming to see Robbie Morgan, chat about the adventure tours business."

She popped the last mouthful of fish in her mouth. "Well, that's nice for Whip."

"Yup."

"I think I'll wash up and take a walk after dinner."

"Dishes fine, walk no. Not alone, anyway."

"I'll take one of the shotguns."

"I'm going into town to take Grace for ice cream, or I'd come with you."

"I'll be fine. I'll strap on my headlamp and load the shotgun. I'm an excellent shot, as you well know."

"Jeez, you better be. Just stay around the stables. Not on the trails."

She gave him a mock salute. "Aye-aye, Captain."

"You're an asshole, sis. You know that don't you?"

"That makes two of us." She smiled, standing and taking their empty plates to the sink. "It's still light. Maybe I'll walk now and clean up after?"

"Good plan."

THE SUN WAS SETTING as she started off up the hill toward the stables. She'd decided to walk the tracks. The larger one was eight furlongs, the smaller one six. If she walked each one, then came back home, she'd have covered about three miles, which she deemed perfect for an evening stroll to walk off dinner. The fact that her route took her past the bunkhouses twice and in sight of them the entire time was an added bonus. *I will not knock on his door*, she told herself as she reached the top of the rise. The stables complex stretched out in front of her, and she marveled, as she always did, at the amazing place she now called home, albeit temporarily. The modern, western-style buildings blended perfectly with their surroundings, the landscaping magnificent. Even in the twilight, one could see the thought and expertise that had gone into the design.

Coyotes howled in the distance as she stepped onto the longer track and began walking southward. Occasionally, she glimpsed movement in the shadows, but no creature showed itself. A short time later as she crossed from one track to the other, she spied him sitting on the fence. Even in the darkness, she recognized the shape of his broad shoulders, the lopsided, worn Stetson, and shoulder-length hair. As Bella approached, he hopped down and came to meet her.

He tipped his hat. "Evenin'."

"Hello. Were you afraid I was a trespasser?" As she looked up at him, he squinted in the beam of the headlamp.

"No, your brother asked me to keep an eye on you."

"You've been watching me the whole time?"

He shrugged.

Bella switched off her headlamp. "Typical."

"No one should be out here alone right now."

She raised her left hand, revealing the shotgun. "I'm fine. I know how to use this, and I have pepper spray in my pocket."

"Probably be useless if a cougar ran at you in the dark."

Instead of arguing, she fell in step with him, and they headed back toward the stables and bunkhouses. "How have you been?"

"Pretty good."

"I hear Patty's treatment of Ghost's mouth is helping."

"Yup."

"Has his temperament improved?"

"Not enough for the bosses to change their mind. There's some guy picking him up at the end of next week."

"Where are they taking him?"

"You don't want to know."

"So sad. He's such a beautiful horse." As they walked, she was acutely conscious of his body as they brushed against each other from time to time. Oh, how she missed him. His touch, his kiss, his warmth.

"Yeah, I'll miss him."

"Tom tells me your folks are coming to visit."

He nodded. "Tomorrow. I'll make sure they meet you. They're staying at Morgan's Run, but they'll be over here a lot. I think they'll be at Harley and Ruthie's barbecue this Friday. You going?"

"Didn't know about it, but if Tom goes, I'll probably tag along. I've been really busy at work, so I have no idea what's going on."

"I hear you." They now stood in front of the bunkhouses. "I can walk you home."

"I'll be fine."

"Well, I'll watch till you get to your porch, then."

"This is silly."

"Cougars are nothing to fool around with."

"I don't mean the cougars. I'm talking about this enforced separation. I've missed you." She moved nearer, taking his hand.

He stepped back. "Let's not push it, okay?"

Bella felt as if she'd been punched. "What's that supposed to mean?"

"It means that my boss isn't crazy about this," he said, waving a hand between them. "And I want to keep my job."

"So that's more important than us?"

"No, of course not, but I'm not sure what I'm doing right now. Maybe after my folks leave, we can see where we are."

"Well, that's just nuts!" she said, her voice angrier than she intended.

"Yup, that's me. Nuts."

"That's not what I meant, and you know it."

"Better head down before it's pitch-black."

"That's it? That's all you have to say?"

"I guess so."

"Fine, good night!" she said and stomped off. *Men,* she thought. *Why do I keep getting sucked into impossible relationships?*

Halfway home, she had the feeling she was being watched, not from behind, but a presence in the brush to the east. A chill threaded up her spine as she reached the porch and quickly climbed the steps. As she opened the door, she turned north toward the stables and saw his silhouette. Momentarily comforted to know he'd been watching, she let herself in and closed the door. *What the hell was that?* she mused as she set the shotgun down beside the door.

CHAPTER 18

"So how are you really, son?" Sara Kittredge's intense violet eyes studied him. Sara, her husband John, and Whip's sister Addie had arrived at Morgan's Run midafternoon. All checked into their rooms, the family were now seated on the Lodge terrace, enjoying a delicious dinner, thanks to George Baran, the ranch's Le Cordon Bleu chef.

"I'm fine, Mom. How are your rooms?"

"Gorgeous. Don't change the subject."

"Leave the boy alone Sary," John Kittredge said. "We've only just arrived. Plenty of time to grill him later."

Addie rolled her eyes. "Watch out, big brother. She's switched into her Gold River Belle mode," she said, referring to their mom's very popular blog about life on an island in the wilderness, complete with her probing interviews of all kinds of people and invited guests.

"Hush," Sara said, running her fingers through her thick dark hair streaked with gray. A handsome woman, she'd created an earth mother online presence, and the persona was pretty accurate. She favored peasant clothes like the muslin blouse and skirt she wore this evening, or jeans and flannel shirts. "I'm just concerned. We haven't heard much from you, Whipster. How are they treating you down here?"

"Great, and please don't use that nickname around other people, especially my bosses. They're amazing, by the way. Couldn't be working for better people. The owners, the big bosses, are terrific too, and incredibly generous."

His father nodded. "They were here to greet us when we arrived. Must be nice to realize your dream with your oldest friend. They're quite a pair, Ben and Spark."

"Sure are. You'll see 'em again Friday night at Harley and Ruthie's, maybe sooner. They're always around."

Once the spotlight was off Whip, they began discussing their plans for the week. Full and sated, they declined dessert. Whip asked his sister if she'd like to go into town for a drink at the Bulldog, which she happily accepted. "Let me just run to the room for my bag," she said, heading for the stairs.

"I'm gonna hit the hay, son," his father said. "See you in the morning. Looking forward to going out to Valley Stables before my meeting with Robbie Morgan."

"Night, Dad." Whip hugged his robust, balding father, who had soft brown eyes, rosy cheeks, and a round nose like Santa. "See you out there."

As he turned to say good night to his mother, she waved her hand at her husband. "You head up. I want to grab something in the gift shop."

John shook his head, knowing full well what she was up to. "No more grilling, sweetie. Let his story unfold. We've got all week."

"Shoo now," she said, waving both hands at him like she was herding sheep. As her husband turned away, she looked up at her son. "Walk you out?"

"I'm waiting for Addie, remember?"

"Then just outside the door. Come on," she said, taking hold of his arm.

"Mom, I know what this is about. I'm doing great."

"First thing we heard when we got in was all the reports about cougars in the area."

"Yeah, and everyone's taking precautions."

"And we hear you've got a girl?"

"Not really. Just a friend."

"That's not what Ben Morgan told me."

Anger raced through his body, and he fought for control. "Then he's mistaken." *Small towns!*

"I'm only saying that after Johnny and Ellie, I know what a trigger even the thought of a mountain lion is to you, sweetheart. You've pushed away every nice young woman because of it. Pushed away closeness to anyone, really."

"That's not true, and I'm handling it. As a matter of fact, I made an appointment with a therapist in town. It's tomorrow. She comes highly recommended."

"That's the best news I've heard in years," she said, squeezing his arm as Addie appeared.

"I'm ready!" his sister said, gazing from mother to brother.

"Great, let's hit it. Night, Mom," he said, giving her a quick peck on the cheek.

"What the hell was that about?" Addie asked as they headed for the truck.

"Mom and the cougar crap. I'm over it," he said, more forcefully than he intended.

"Well, we all know that's not true," she said, following him. "But let's stick it in a box for tonight. I want to hear all about the Valley scene, especially any single, handsome cowboys."

Whip laughed, waiting for her to catch up. He put his arm around her. "Well, you've come to the right place for that. Men outnumber women three to one."

"Whoopee!"

"Good to have you here, sis."

"Good to be here, big brother."

LONELY AND LISTLESS, Bella threw herself into a busy workday. Wednesdays were the free clinic. Women for miles around, mostly those without health insurance, came in for all kinds of wellness and pregnancy issues, so she was kept busy attending to their needs. At the end of the day, she bumped into Marc Koenig.

He gazed down at her with pale blue eyes. "Hey, Bella, how've you been?"

"Busy and you?"

"Same here."

It was on the tip of her tongue to ask if he'd like to grab a drink sometime when he leaned over and whispered, "I've got a date tonight."

"Really? How nice for you. Do I know the lucky lady?"

"Her name's Haley Alvarez. She's a therapist in town. You may have heard of her? We met at the Community Center square dance a couple of weeks ago. She's a great person."

"That's wonderful. I'm happy for you," Bella said. "I've heard Haley's name before, but never met her."

"We'll remedy that soon, maybe at the annual office barbecue."

"Well, have a good evening."

"You are too. Anything special?"

"Scrabble night at the CC."

"Win big," he said as they parted company.

"Thanks."

"WHY SO GLUM?" Grace asked as the two women stacked chairs and folded tables at the end of Scrabble. "You didn't seem on top of your game tonight."

"Discouraged, that's all. I'll tell you later."

"Want to head over to the Bulldog for a quick drink? I've gotta check on Dad, as you know."

"Love to."

After checking on Wilbur, who was in the back room playing cards with three friends, each of them ordered a Saguaro Vineyard

Pinot Noir and sat at the bar. "Thank God for those guys," Grace said. "So, what's up with you?"

"It's the whole saga with Whip. One minute we're on, the next he's running in the opposite direction. It's an emotional roller coaster. Then there's my brother hovering all over me and probably threatening Whip too."

Grace smiled at her friend as she patted Bella's hand. "I haven't heard about any threatening, and they seem like they're good buddies when I'm there working with Dusty. Tom told me Whip's folks were in town. Maybe he's preoccupied with that?"

"Maybe, but it doesn't feel like that. He's also completely incommunicado. You'd think if he cared two hoots about me, he'd at least shoot a quick text. Do you know that I was even considering flirting with my boss, Marc Koenig? Do you know him?"

"Yeah, real nice guy. He comes into the hardware store sometimes. He lost his wife a few years ago. She was a wonderful person. He'd be a good catch."

"Well, he's taken, so that's the end of that," Bella said glumly.

"Uh-oh." Grace's gaze was directed behind her friend.

"What?" Bella asked, turning around to observe Whip and an auburn-haired beauty, sliding out of a booth and heading their way. *So that's why he's in the wind. Where did she come from?* she thought as the pair reached them.

"Evenin', ladies," Whip said, looking from one to the other of them.

"Hi, Whip," Grace said.

"Hi," Bella echoed her friend.

"This is my sister, Addie. She's here with my folks for a week. Addie, this is Grace, my boss's fiancée and a budding horse whisperer, and this is Bella, my boss's sister. She's a midwife in town."

Addie smiled. "Pleased to meet you both. I've been quizzing my big brother about eligible cowboys in town, but he's been relatively unspecific."

Grace laughed. "Oh, they're around. Are you going to Harley and Ruthie's Friday night?"

"Yup," Whip said.

"There will been a hoard of them there," Grace said.

"Well, shall we Addie?" he asked, indicating the door.

"You're welcome to join us. We're just having a quick drink before I haul my dad out of here," Grace said.

"That'd be great!" Addie said.

"Sorry, sis, no can do. I've got to be up really early in the morning."

Addie gave him a quizzical look, then shrugged. "Okay, I guess we're going. Great to meet you both. Hope to see you around."

As he herded her out the door, Grace and Bella heard Addie say, "I thought you said you were sleeping in tomorrow?"

Bella gave her friend a look. "See what I mean? I'm the plague, and he's running from it."

"That's not true. He's probably just caught up in family stuff. She's cute, his sister, huh?"

"She is at that. She better wear body armor Friday night. They'll be swarming all over her."

They sat a few more minutes drinking and chatting until Grace noticed her father standing up, presumably headed to the bar for another drink. "That's my cue," she said as she intercepted him. "Hey, Dad, care to walk two ladies home on the mean streets of Saguaro?"

His eyes narrowed, but instead of arguing, he said, "Lemme just tell the fellas I'm going."

They walked Bella back to the Community Center lot, then said good night. As she drove back home to Valley Stables, Bella wondered if things would ever become clear where Whip was concerned. *Maybe I'd better check out the cowboys Friday myself,* she mused as she parked alongside the farmhouse.

"Hey, sis," Tom said, from his porch rocker. He often ended the night on the porch, watching the stars come out. "Sorry I missed Scrabble. How'd you do?"

"So so. Grace and I stopped at the Bulldog after." She sat in the adjacent rocker, gazing up at the stars.

"Oh yeah? I could have joined you, darn it. Our meeting ended an hour ago. Too late for Scrabble, never too late for the Bulldog. How was Wilbur?"

"Okay. He was playing cards and didn't seem drunk."

"Good."

"We ran into Whip and his sister, Addie. Have you met her yet?"

He shook his head. "I will tomorrow when they get the grand tour, I guess."

"She seems really nice."

"Uh-huh. What about her brother?"

Bella stood abruptly. "I'm going to bed. Night, Tommy."

"Night. Sorry if I hit a nerve."

"You didn't," she lied. "I'm fine." *Like I'm fooling anyone!*

CHAPTER 19

Thursday morning Whip gave his parents a tour of the stables,, then John, Sara and Addie headed into town to meet with Robbie at Valley Outdoor Adventures. His parents encouraged Whip to take his time collecting them as they wanted to stroll around town, wander through Saguaro Dreams, and stop in at Rambler Sports and talk with the owner, Lang Dillon, Robbie's brother-in-law. After he dropped them at the Main Street office, Whip parked and headed to Haley Alvarez's.

The short, round therapist with waist-length, curly silver hair greeted him in the plant-filled outer office, her eyes warm. Barefoot, she was dressed in black leggings and a flowing tunic, its silken fabric swirled with the colors of the earth.

"Come in, come in. You must be Whip."

"Yes, hello," he said, fighting a strong urge to turn tail and run. It wasn't the woman. He instantly felt comfortable with her kind presence. No, it was the journey they were about to take. He took a deep breath and followed her into the inner room furnished with two overstuffed chairs and a love seat. She waved him into one of the chairs. "Can I get you something to drink? Tea? Water?"

"Water would be great, thanks."

She stooped and retrieved two water bottles from a small fridge in the corner, handed him one and then sat in the other chair. "I'm glad to meet you, Whip Kittredge. Now how can I help?"

He gulped, unsure of how to begin. "I'm not sure where to begin, but I decided to come to see you specifically because I'm having trouble in a relationship with a woman for whom I care deeply, maybe even love. I'm pretty sure the freakouts I've been having are related to a past trauma."

"Freakouts?"

"One minute, I'm pulling her closer, the next, I'm shoving her away. Anytime I get close to anyone, especially women, I tend to cut and run."

"And you think it's related to the past?"

He nodded.

"Are you the only one aware of this past trauma?"

Surprised, he met her eyes. "No, it was a tragedy for my whole family."

"Is it something you can talk about?"

He gave her a wan smile. "I can try, but if I turn to stone, don't be surprised."

She smiled. "Thanks for the warning. Please, tell me as much as is comfortable for you."

"I grew up on Vancouver Island. My dad was a logger, and we lived out in the middle of nowhere. When he married my mom, it was a second marriage and he brought two kids with him, my stepbrother, Johnny, and stepsister, Ellie. Johnny was seven years older than me and Ellie five years older. I worshipped them, especially Johnny.

"When I was about five and Johnny was twelve, and Ellie ten, we decided to go on an adventure. My mom was heavily pregnant, or she probably would have tagged along, but she packed us lunch and lectured Ellie and Johnny about looking out for me. We had a lot of wildlife all around us—deer, grizzlies, coyotes, and cougars—but it had been a quiet summer and wildlife usually didn't frequent that part of the island.

"We headed out shortly before noon and hiked for an hour or so.

We were headed toward Lizard Pond. They have a nice beach and a lifeguard, so Mom knew we'd be safe. The trail was narrow, and we were in thick forest. Ellie was behind me and Johnny in the lead." Whip gazed down and realized his hands were trembling and water was spilling from his bottle onto the carpeted floor.

"Oh, gee, sorry," he said, setting it on a nearby table.

"No worries at all. Would you like to take a break?"

"I'm okay. Might as well get this over with."

By the time he reached the end of his description, Whip's face was wet with tears, and he trembled from head to toe. "Sorry," he said.

Haley came to kneel in front of his chair, then wrapped her arms around him. "You're safe now."

"Maybe if I'd stayed?" he said, voicing the fear he'd held in his heart for twenty-five years.

"You were five years old," she said softly. "It sounds like there was nothing you could have done, and this was certainly not your fault." She handed him a box of tissues, then stood and returned to her seat.

"I've never told any of this to anyone. I mean, they knew what happened, but not how or what I saw."

"That's a huge burden to carry."

"What do you think? Am I a hopeless case?" he asked as he mopped tears from his cheeks.

"Hardly. We could take more time now, but I'm going to suggest that we stop for today and that you rest and come back tomorrow. I have time in the morning before nine. Anytime from six to nine. Or late afternoon?"

"Morning's better for me. Would seven work?"

"Seven it is."

"I'll speak to my boss. I'm sure it won't be a problem, but if it is, I'll call."

As he stood up and tossed his empty water bottle into a waste basket, Haley rose and laid her hand gently on his arm. "One of the things that happens with trauma like yours is that people, you in this case, may assume that if they talk about it, they'll lose their hold on sanity. So they stay silent, not letting anyone get close so they never have to speak of the past and such a horrific event. Casual friendships are fine, but intimacy requires that we reveal ourselves, our deep selves, our sufferings, and our joys. In the end, however, we come to realize that there is healing and comfort in sharing, even if it seems terrifying."

He shrugged. "Maybe."

"Telling our stories is the first step in letting go of pain. The first step in healing and becoming whole. Sharing with those who love us can help us to find peace."

"If you say so," he said, turning to go. "See you at seven tomorrow."

Haley nodded. "Yes. Take good care till then."

THE MINUTE SARA KITTREDGE spotted her son, she could tell he'd been through hell and back. "Hey, honey, you okay?" she asked while the others found a table at Gracie's Diner.

"Getting there."

Her violet eyes studied him. "Want to talk about it?"

"I told her."

"Good."

"I'm seeing her again in the morning."

"I'm glad," she said, taking his arm. "Now, your dad and sister have found us a booth. Let's order some food, which I hear is incredible."

"It is," he said. "It really is."

All four of them ordered Gracie Burgers with extra sauce. It was the diner owner's specialty. People begged her for the recipe, but she refused to divulge it, even to her niece, Grace McGraw, or her brother, Wilbur. Maria, the waitress, brought them waters and iced teas and hurried off to the kitchen with the order.

"So how was your morning?" Whip asked his dad. "Did you get lots of good tips?"

"Did we ever. And that Dillon fella has quite an operation going too."

They spent the meal discussing what they'd learned from Robbie and Lang and thoughts they had for the future. After lunch, Whip dropped them at the Lodge. Both Addie and her mom had appointments at the adjacent spa for massages and pedicures and John said after his big lunch he needed a nap.

"But we do want to come out and see the mustangs, see what you've been doing with that stallion."

"What time should I pick you up? It's almost one now."

"How about we come to you?" his father said. "We've got our fancy rented SUV, and I'm sure between GPS and the Lodge concierge, we can find our way back out there. Is four too late?"

"Perfect," Whip said. "Ghost'll be tired then, so he might be less ornery."

As they disembarked in front of the Lodge, Sara came around to hug her son. "Love you, honey. See you soon."

"Thanks, Mom, love you too."

As he drove back through town and headed north to Valley Stables, Whip was surprised at how calm he felt...*now that I've returned from hell.*

CHAPTER 20

"He's doing pretty good today," Tom said. He watched Whip lead and Ghost follow behind him. "This is impressive, buddy. Maybe I should get Harley down here to see this."

Whip turned and put up his hand, the halt signal, twirling the end of the lead a few times to encourage Ghost to back up. "He could just as easily decide to bolt. Hope he behaves when my folks get here."

"Hey, guys," Bella said, emerging from the barn and strolling up to join them. The minute she saw Whip's face, she knew something was terribly wrong. For one thing, his normally tan face was pale, his eyes furtive, brow furrowed. She wondered if the horse could sense his trainer was in distress and decided to be cooperative.

Brother and sister continued to watch man and horse, making the occasional comment while trying not to rattle Ghost. Grace had taken Dusty on a short ride up to the stables and around the larger track, which was vacant at this time of day. They suddenly appeared to the west, threading their way down an old cart trail. As they came alongside the round pen, Ghost snorted and reared, but Whip raised his hand and gently coaxed him down.

"He has no fear, does he?" Bella whispered to her brother.

"Whip or Ghost?"

"Both, but I was referring to Whip."

"Yeah, he's pretty fearless."

As Grace and Dusty disappeared into the barn below, Ghost settled down. Five minutes later, the Kittredges drove up. "Give him a break till they get up here," Tom said. "I'll go meet 'em."

Alone for a few minutes while Ghost went to the water trough, Bella called, "How are you doing?"

Whip strolled across the pen to where she stood. "I'm okay. Sorry I haven't been in touch."

"You look tired," she said softly.

"It's been a rough day," he said, refusing to meet her gaze. He looked over her toward the barn and waved to his family as they made their way over to them. "Better get back to Ghost. Fingers crossed that he behaves himself."

Bella wanted to say more, but he walked away as his family drew near.

"Hey, Bella!" Addie called. "Good to see you again. These are our parents, Sara and John. Mom and Dad, this is Bella."

After they all shook hands, they positioned themselves along the fence to watch Whip and Ghost. "Well now, would you look at that," John Kittredge said. "He's always been good with horses, but mostly riding them."

"He's doing an amazing job," Tom said. "All in his off hours. The bosses have decided not to keep Ghost, but your son's not giving up till the last second."

"What will happen to him?" Addie said.

"Nothing you want to know about."

"They'll send him to a slaughterhouse, I expect," Sara said. "Either south of the border or overseas. Poor animal. He's too beautiful for such a fate. They should've left him on the range."

Tom shrugged. "Done now. Too late to return him to the wild. He wouldn't last long without his herd."

They watched for a while longer, then Tom called, "Better cool him down before he gets testy. I'll take him in. You visit with your folks."

"But I should—" Whip started.

Tom raised his hand. "No buts about it. Go have fun with your family." With that, Tom jumped into the round pen and picked up Ghost's lead, "Hey, boy. Let's get you inside for dinner."

Whip climbed over the fence, gazing at his parents. "What d'you think?"

"Very impressive, son," his father said.

"We're so proud of you, honey," Sara said, hugging him.

"Pretty cool, bro," Addie said, giving him a thumbs-up.

"Are you able to eat with us, honey?" his mother asked. "We've been asked to dine at Spark Foster's, which is very kind of them. Just us, Ben and Leonora Morgan, and Spark. Addie's not sure what she's going to do. Not too thrilled to eat with the old fogies or at the Lodge."

"Thanks, but I think I'll stay around here tonight," he said. "Addie's welcome to come eat with the bunkhouse crew."

"I accept!" his sister said, clapping her hands. "Will you be there, Bella?"

Bella smiled. She enjoyed watching the interactions between what was clearly a loving family and was surprised at Addie's question. "No, I haven't had that pleasure yet, but I hear the food's good."

"But she could come, couldn't she?" Addie turned to her brother.

"Sure, if you want," he replied.

Observing Whip's expression, it was clear to Bella that her coming to dinner was the last thing he wanted. "Thanks, but I have plans with a friend tonight." Keenly aware that Whip's parents had been witness to this uncomfortable scene, she said, "In fact, I'll let you go. I just got home from work, as you can see." She waved her hands, indicating her scrubs, the fabric a bright, colorful print. "Gotta run up to the house and get changed. Enjoy your evening!"

With that, she headed off, taking the narrow path behind the paddocks that led to the farmhouse.

"She's a lovely young woman, your Bella," Sara said, studying her son.

"Yeah, she's great, but she's not my Bella, Mom."

"And we believe that, don't we?" Addie whispered to Sara as they headed for the barn.

"Hey, sis," Whip called. "It's gonna be about an hour before I'm through here. You can either hang or help me and the guys bring in the mustangs."

"Put me to work!" she said.

"You sure you're okay, son?" Sara asked.

"Leave him be," her husband said. "Now come on, or we'll be late for dinner with the fogies."

"I'm fine, Mom. Enjoy your dinner. Spark's Casa Grande is pretty spectacular, and his chef is amazing." *Yeah right, I'm fine all right*, he thought, waving to Addie to follow him to the big corral.

Later, when he and Addie walked up to the bunkhouse dining room, he saw Bella's SUV parked beside the farmhouse. He guessed that she and Tom were both home tonight and her begging out of dinner was a lie. *Won't tell Addie, though*, he mused while she chattered away beside him.

"So, your boyfriend's doing fine work with Ghost," Tom said, gazing across the dinner table at his sister.

"He's not my boyfriend, but yes, he's making progress. You think Harley, Ben, and Spark will change their minds?"

"Doubtful. They're looking at the big picture, and Ghost is taking a lot of time with one of the ranch's best wranglers. I've been covering for Whip because it looks like he really needs this win, but don't think they don't notice."

"So, you sense something's wrong too?"

Her brother raised his eyebrow, giving her a look. "I may seem like a stupid cowboy—"

"Hardly."

"I may seem like a dumb cowboy, but I do have a heart, and I know when something's troubling one of my crew."

"He looked like a mess just now," she said. "I wonder if something happened. With his folks maybe?"

"Or maybe it has to do with a certain young gal he's crazy about? What's going on with you two anyway?"

"Darned if I know. One minute, he's there, the next, hundreds of miles away. You want any more?" she asked, looking over at the pile of bones on his plate.

"Wish I could fit more, but I'm happy to have the leftovers for lunch tomorrow."

Bella stood, taking both of their plates to the sink. "I'll wrap the leftovers and leave the dishes until after my walk."

"You know I don't think these walks are a good idea."

"I'll wear my headlamp and bring the shotgun. I'll be fine. A cougar's not going to jump the fence around the track, and I think I can make it back and forth from there to here unscathed."

"Famous last words. Be careful is all. I'm going down to check the barn, then I'll be here. Grace is coming over to hang out. Cards, TV, something."

"I'll steer clear of the something and go straight to my room upon my return. No worries." She stowed the platter of ribs covered in tinfoil in the fridge.

"Ha-ha. I'll wash up."

As it was a clear night, Bella walked up to the stables, the occasional call of a hawk or screech of an owl piercing the silence from time to time. If the coyotes were around, they had not yet begun to howl, and the occasional rustling and snuffling sounds in the brush sounded like javelinas. As she passed the bunkhouses, Whip stepped out, tipping his hat, but taking a position in the shadows rather than approaching her.

"Tom called you, didn't he?" she said.

"Yup."

"Well, don't just stand there. If you're supposed to be protecting me, you might as well walk with me."

He hesitated for a minute, then strolled over to join her.

"Where's Addie?"

"Greg drove her home. He insisted. They're in love."

"Lucky them," she said as they walked side by side toward the corral.

"Yup."

They fell silent as they entered the gate of the larger track and began walking north. The sky was thick with stars and the fireflies were out, surrounding them as they rounded the track.

"Like the stars have come down from the sky," he said.

Surprised, she stopped and faced him. "Yes, they're beautiful. Now are you going to tell me what's going on?"

"Nope."

"Why not? Wouldn't it help to talk about it?"

"Not now, Bella. I'm sorry."

She was just about to protest when he pulled her to him and captured her lips in a deep, searing kiss. As she gave herself to him, Bella felt her knees buckling and wondered if she might actually fall over. Just as suddenly, he released her, breaking the kiss, but holding her arm as if he sensed her unsteadiness.

"What was that?" she asked, her voice thick with sensation.

"Just wanted you to know that that's still what I want and I'm taking steps to get there. Come on, let's keep walking before the mosquitoes start swarming." He pulled her along, and they reached the gate without another word.

When they stood in front of the bunkhouse, he asked, "Want me to walk you down?"

"Is that all you have to say?"

"Yup."

"You're exasperating, Whip Kittredge. I hope you realize that."

"Yup."

"Aren't you going to kiss me good night?"

He paused, then said, "I think I will." He drew her close, but this time, the kiss was short and sweet. After, he held her in his arms for several minutes. When he finally let go, he whispered, "Thanks."

"For?"

"For maybe not giving up on me yet?"

In the lights of the bunkhouse and stables, she could see his eyes had filled with tears. She reached up and touched his cheek. "Never. And I hope someday you'll let me in, let me help."

He took her hand and kissed her palm. "My problem, my responsibility."

She wanted to argue, but instead, said, "Good night, then."

"Night, Bella."

As she made her way down the hill, she once again had the sensation that she was being watched, and not by the man behind her. The hairs on the back of her neck stood up as she ran to the porch steps, turning to wave before she opened and closed the door. As she set the shotgun against the wall, back against the door, she spied two surprised faces observing her. Tom and Grace sat on the sofa staring, his arm draped around his fiancee's shoulders.

He grabbed the remote and clicked off the television. "What's wrong, Belle? You're white as a sheet."

She plunked down in a chair beside them. "This is the second time I've felt like something or someone was watching from the brush. It's really creepy."

"That settles it. No more walking alone. Didn't Whip walk you to the door?"

"He offered to walk me down, but I told him not to bother. He watched till I reached the door."

"Well, unless he walks you to the door, no more walking at night. Jeez."

Bella suddenly noticed Grace, who had been quietly watching the interactions between brother and sister. "Hi, Grace. Good to see you."

"You too. Tom's right, you do look pale. It's scary out there with all the mountain lion talk. My dad claims coyotes sometimes hunt in packs too."

"Well, I'm fine, and I'll let you guys get back to your show. I'm off to bed." She gave them both quick hugs, went to the kitchen for a glass of water, then headed upstairs. "Don't worry about me. I'm a sound sleeper," she called from the landing.

CHAPTER 21

Friday, Whip's parents drove to Tucson for lunch with old friends. Addie stayed behind and spent the morning at Valley Adventures shadowing Robbie and his crew. After another session with Haley, Whip put in a full morning up and down, from mustangs to thoroughbreds, then headed into town to get lunch for the crew. He picked Addie up, and brother and sister walked the short distance to Gracie's with Robbie and his partner, Hal Garard. They parted inside the door, Robbie and Hal to a table and Whip and Addie to the counter to pick up large bags of food and drinks. "Hey, you going to my sister's tonight?" Robbie asked.

"Yup, bringing the whole family."

"Great, see you there, then."

"Thanks for this morning," Addie said, looking at Hal. "It was really helpful to see you guys in action. Wish I could stay and go on one of your trips."

"Any time," Hal said, flashing a hundred-watt smile, his dark eyes twinkling.

"Leaving poor Greg in the dust already?" Whip whispered.

"Oh, you're hilarious, brother dear. Come on, let's get the food. I'm starving."

"You're always starving."

They both grabbed two bags, and Whip headed for the door.

"Don't you have to pay?"

"They run a tab."

As they stowed the food in his truck, Bella came down the sidewalk from the park where she'd eaten lunch.

Addie waved. "Hi, Bella!"

"Hi, Kittredges!" she said, pausing.

Whip tipped his hat. "Hey."

Addie stared at her companions, a puzzled look on her face. Finally, she broke the silence with "We've just picked up enough food to feed an army. You going home soon? You could eat with the crew."

"Lucky crew... The food, I mean. Thanks, but I just ate, and I've got patients all afternoon. Are you enjoying your stay in Saguaro?"

"It's awesome. Spent the morning with Robbie and his guys. What a great place that is. If Dad didn't need me, I'd be tempted to move down here and beg for a job."

Whip stood awkwardly by as they chatted about Valley Adventures. When there was a break in the conversation, he said, "We better get this food back."

"Of course," Bella said. "I'll see you both tonight, then?"

"Sure will!" Addie said, hopping into the truck.

One more hat tip and Whip got into the truck. "See ya, Bella."

As they drove out of town, Addie turned to him. "What was that? You guys are crazy about each other. Anyone can see that. So why the weird behavior?"

"Don't want to talk about it," he said, as they headed north on the Gila Highway.

MOUNTAINS OF FOOD were already laid out on tables along the third-floor deck when Tom, Grace, and Bella walked into his boss's home. Ruthie called hello from the kitchen, and Bella turned to her brother. "I'm going to check and see if she needs any help."

"I'll come too," Grace said. "Let the cowboys connect."

Tom nodded. "Have fun. Give a yell if I can carry things out."

Dressed in a frilly apron, their hostess moved back and forth from the small third-floor kitchen to the deck, each time with bowls and platters of food. "Hey, gals."

"What can we do?" Grace asked.

"It's a bigger crowd tonight. My parents and Spark came to keep the Kittredges company. This means my mom had Carmela cooking all day, and she's brought a ton of stuff. Mom's downstairs in the big kitchen sending all the food up the dumb waiter. She's obsessed with the dumb waiter. If you want to help, bring things out to the deck. That'd be great."

"Where are the kids?" Bella asked as they went back and forth from the small galley kitchen carrying enough food to feed the entire town.

"Willow's home with two friends. They've got them somewhere." Sure enough, at that moment, Harley's oldest daughter ran through the room chasing Charlotte and Pickles, Lily Dillon in hot pursuit, followed by Willow's two college friends. One, a tall brunette, looked into it, the blonde behind her looked ready to bolt. Bella smiled. *Probably more interested in the cowboys everywhere*, she thought.

Finally, Bella and Grace wandered off in one direction, Ruthie in the other, saying she needed to check on Admiral Leonora downstairs. "If my kids are in trouble, call my husband, would you?" she said as she headed down the stairs.

They found Tom on the lower terrace talking to Whip's parents and Ben Morgan senior. The latter's grandson, Ben the third, tore by, running after his buddy Jasper Larrabee, son of Kevin Larrabee, a successful local contractor married to Polly, the head teacher at the Morgan's Run Cottage nursery and day care. Jasper and Bennie were the same age. Both had entered kindergarten the previous fall and were known as holy terrors, as they had been during their Cottage years.

"Hellions," Ben Senior said, shaking his head. "I wonder where they're off to now."

"They're adorable," Sara Kittredge said. "And so lucky to be growing up in this magical place."

"Sure are," Spark Foster said, nodding as he joined them, handing Sara a white wine. "Now if we could just drive the mountain lions back into the mountains where they belong, we could breathe more easily. I wanted you to meet my daughter Amy and her little family, but they're away visiting Jeb's parents up north. He works for Maggie at the stables, and they have two kids, Toby and a newborn, Spencer Jake Barnes. They're calling him Jake after Jeb's dad. Bella delivered him. She's a miracle worker."

"Sure is." Ben nodded. "And the baby boom continues," Ben said. "Guess that's inevitable with our big families."

"Who is that beautiful woman with the infant on her hip?" Sara asked.

Ben smiled. "That's our Maggie. Runs the stables at the ranch, and she's married to our oldest, Ben. A great gal. She's holding Cora, our newest grandchild, born just after little Pickles."

"Is that her daughter walking beside her?"

"Yup. Emma. She's my sweetheart."

As they observed mother and daughters, Ben Morgan the second joined them, slipping his arm around Maggie's shoulders.

"That's my son," Ben said, grinning.

"Oh my, he's gorgeous. How many kids do you have?"

"Six," the family patriarch said. "Four sons, but only Ben and Robbie live here. Sam's in Baltimore and Kyle's in New England. We miss 'em like crazy. Our daughters Beth and Ruthie live here. They run the ranch's farm. Did you get out there yet?"

"No, but we'd love to see it," John said as his wife nodded.

"We'll make sure that happens," Ben said. "You've met Ruthie, our hostess tonight, and that's our oldest daughter, Bethie. She's holding little Tucker, and his big sister Lily just flew by with the pack. I'm glad you got to see her husband Lang's operation. He's been very successful out here with Rambler Sports West."

Bella excused herself and wandered off to say hello to Maggie, as did Grace and Tom. As the group continued to converse, Sara spotted her son coming down the steps from above. His eyes scanned the crowd until he spotted Bella. Spark noticed her gaze and said, "What do you think, Mama? Will those two ever get together?"

Surprised, Sara turned and looked up at him. "Oh Spark, darned if I know. My son's sure not telling me anything."

The tall sixty-four-year-old draped his arm around her shoulders. "If it's meant to be, they'll find a way."

"Food's ready," Ruthie called from above, her handsome husband beside her. "Grab a plate, refresh your drink, and prepare to eat a lot! Harley's cooked every kind of meat you can think of, and his ribs are to die for."

"Well, who can say no to that?" John said. The group made their way toward the stairs.

In the rush to fill plates and find places to eat, no one except Sara noticed Bella and Whip greet each other and walk together in the opposite direction, skirting the herd of kids running in from the playground.

CHAPTER 22

"Hi," Bella said. "Great party."

"They always are," Whip said, giving her a shy smile.

"How are things going?"

"They're going."

"Your folks seem to be having a great time."

"Yeah, much more of this and they'll be making noises about moving to Saguaro.

They're going to have to drag my sister away," he said when they passed Addie chatting with Hal Garard and Robbie. "Poor Greg's been left in the dust now that she's met handsome Hal."

As they talked, the couple wandered past the play yard with its swings, slides, jungle gym, and seesaw, around one of two barns, the farthest from the house. Now out of sight of the party, he turned to her. "I've missed you."

"We were together last night, if you recall."

"Yeah, confused, screwed up together."

"So, what about tonight? More of the same," she said, gazing up, her hands on his chest. She had on a thin summer dress, the neckline affording a lovely view of her cleavage.

He shrugged, hands on her arms, keeping her at bay. "Not sure, but I wanted to talk to you alone."

"I'm glad," she whispered, smiling. "What did you want to talk about?"

"I wanted to tell you I'm trying to deal with my messed-up self and Haley has been great. We've made a bunch more appointments over the next month."

"Good, I'm happy for you. Anything else?" she asked, her voice silky soft.

"Only that I'm burning up inside wanting to make love to you right here, right now."

"Well, what's stopping you? We wouldn't want you to combust, would we? I am wearing a dress."

"Oh hell, Bella," he said, his voice gruff as he pulled her to him, capturing her lips in a deep, luscious kiss, lots of tongue.

Before she knew what was happening, his hands cupped her breasts, then moved south as he lifted her skirt and slipped off her panties. His fingers moved between his legs, finding her hot and moist as he caressed her clit. Panting now, she was almost delirious with wanting him. Her fingers moved down from his chest to the hard bulge in his jeans, and she unzipped and released him, stroking.

"Oh baby." He lifted her and wrapped her beautiful legs around him. "You ready?"

In answer, she released his cock and guided it inside her. "Take me, cowboy. Give me the ride of my life."

Whip plunged into her, and they began their frenzied, wild love-making, her back pressed against the rough barn wall. As they rose to a thundering climax, they heard voices nearby, children's voices. "Shit," he mumbled, carrying her around the corner, then pulling out of her and setting her gently on the ground.

He quickly zipped his jeans, then looked up. "Shit, your panties. They're back there."

Bella smiled. "They won't notice."

"Hell they won't," he said. He sneaked around the corner and ran to retrieve the lacy white underwear. The kids were on the swings and jungle gym, involved in their games, and appeared not to notice him.

Bella pulled on her panties and leaned against the barn. "Do I look okay?"

"Beautiful."

"No, I'm serious. Do I look like I've been... I mean, you know what I mean. Will people guess what we've been doing?"

Suddenly, he was laughing. His warm eyes shone as he pulled her close. "I doubt the kids will guess what we've been up to, at least. To everyone else? Excuse my language, but you look as if you've been well f—"

Before he could say the word, she pressed her fingers to his lips. "Don't even say it. Should I go hide in the car?"

He took her hand. "Come on, let's eat. By the time we get to the food, your glow might have worn off."

"Very funny."

"Hurry up. Before my mom sends out a search party."

"Whip?" she asked as they headed for the corner of the barn. "That was incredible."

He smiled, pulling her to him, kissing her gently. "Sure was. I promise I'm going to keep trying."

As they rounded the barn, Ben and Jasper ran up to them. "What'cha doin', Whip?" Ben asked, gazing up with his dark brown eyes.

"Just taking a walk, buddy," Whip said, ruffling his hair.

As Whip and Bella headed for the house holding hands, they heard Jasper say, "They weren't walking. They've been doing what Dad and Mommy do when they lock their door."

Bella looked at him. "We're going to hear about this. I guarantee it."

"Yup," he said, dropping her hand and pulling her against him so they walked arm in arm to the stairs.

"Guess we're going public, then?"

"Looks like it. Hope your brother doesn't kill me."

"No worries, he's over it." She spied Tom frowning in their direction as they climbed the porch stairs.

"Well, well, well," Addie said when her brother passed by with Bella.

"Not a word, sis."

From the picnic table below, Sara also noticed the couple and said to her husband, "I think I should have a talk with Bella, don't you?"

"I think you should stay out of it, honey, as I've been saying since we got here."

"We'll see," she whispered, taking a forkful of salad. "By the way," she added, voice louder. "This is one of the most delicious meals I've ever had." Sara smiled and gazed around the table at their companions, Ben, Leonora, and Spark, as well as Lang, Beth, and their children.

CHAPTER 23

The weekend flew by, with Whip showing his parents around the area in between his work at the stables. Monday morning, Sara made a decision. She would not ask her son for Bella's cell number. Instead, she called Valley Ob-Gyn and asked to speak to her.

Bella came on after several minutes. "Hello?"

"Hi, dear. It's Sara Kittredge. As you may know, we're heading home tomorrow, and I didn't want to leave without speaking with you."

"Oh?"

"I know this is a strange request, but I can tell you're very important to my son. Are you free at all to meet with me?"

"When did you have in mind?" Bella asked.

"Whenever's best for you."

"I have a pretty full day, but I do take a break at lunchtime. I could meet you in the park in town. We can find a bench in the shade."

"Perfect. Why don't I pick up some lunch for us? I could ask them to make us some sandwiches here at the Lodge. They have everything. What would you like?"

"A BLT, if they have it. Otherwise, I'll eat anything. Shall we say twelve thirty in the park?"

"Thank you, Bella. This means a lot to me."

"Of course." Bella set down the phone and shook her head. *What next?* she thought as she headed down the hall to her next patient.

AT TWELVE FIFTEEN, Bella closed her office door and headed out to stroll the four blocks to the town green. The beautiful greenspace had been created years earlier, shortly after they paved Main Street, but had never been given a name. Thus, locals referred to it as the park. When she reached the western edge, she spied Whip's mom across the green sitting in the shade of a mimosa tree. Sara waved as she approached, then stood up, reaching out her arms.

"Thank you for coming, dear."

Bella returned her embrace. "Thank you in advance for lunch. A nice treat."

Sandwiches and bottles of water sat neatly between them. "Both the same—BLTs on whole wheat—so take your pick."

They unwrapped their sandwiches and ate a few bites in silence, observing people playing, sitting, and walking around the park. Finally, Sara sighed, putting down her half-eaten sandwich. "What a beautiful spot, and I haven't had a bad meal since we arrived. You're so lucky."

Bella smiled. Even though Whip favored his dad in looks, there was something about this strong, handsome woman, an essence that was so like her son's. "Yes, we are."

"So, I'm sure you're wondering what this is about," Sara said, violet eyes meeting Bella's own.

"A little," Bella said, setting her sandwich down beside her.

"I would never have thought to do this with most gals, and my son's dated a few, but you're different. I can see the way he looks at you. He's in love with you, my dear, even if he's unable to express it. I know because he's never worked so hard to get better with anyone else—not friends, lovers, or his family."

"Get better? I'm not sure I understand. Is he sick?"

"I'm referring to the therapy. He's been seeing a woman in town."

Bella nodded. "Hayley."

"Yes, that's the name. My family experienced a horrible tragedy when Whip was five. It left all of us scarred, but Whip perhaps the most. My husband's strong, and we have each other to lean on. I was carrying Addie, so she was spared."

Bella realized she'd been holding her breath, fearful of what Sara might say, so she slowly let it out and told herself to breathe.

"I'm John's second wife. He's almost ten years older than I am. His first brief marriage fell apart because she couldn't stand island life. We met when he came to San Francisco on a business trip. I was waitressing at one of the waterfront bars, and he asked me out. Says he knew immediately that he wanted to marry me and take me back to the island. I was eighteen. We had a couple of dates, he proposed, and off I went to live on Vancouver Island in the middle of nowhere. A year later, Whip was born. Shortly after his birth, John's ex-wife, Myra, died in a car accident, and their two children, Johnny and Ellie came to live with us full-time.

"It was a heady time with him starting the new company, me raising three kids and going to college part-time, but we did it. I was too young to realize I didn't have a clue what I was doing. We were happy. Our little fractured family slowly healed and became one. Whip idealized his older siblings, and they were wonderful with him. Caring and protective, the best stepkids a mom could have."

"Did you have to commute to the mainland for college?" Bella asked.

"No, I went to Vancouver Island University. It's a great school. Whip started there, then transferred. Anyway... John and I decided to have one more child when Whip was four, and lo and behold, I got pregnant.

"One really hot summer day, the kids begged to go on an adventure to Lizard Cove. I was particularly uncomfortable, heavily pregnant and cranky, so there was no way I wanted to hike over there. I offered to drive them, but they were determined to have a wilderness adventure. They were all good swimmers, even Whip, and the pond's little beach has a full-time lifeguard, so I agreed. When Johnny proposed they take a shortcut through the woods rather than walking on the road, I thought it would be fine. That area was their backyard, and they knew it inside and out. It was stupid of me to let them go, but Johnny was a very mature twelve and Ellie a responsible ten-year-old, so I said yes. I should have made him take the shotgun, but it was broad daylight and there were three of them. I thought it would be safe. The lifeguard station has a phone, so I asked them to call me when they got there and also if they wanted me to pick them up after swimming."

Bella gazed up and saw that Sara's cheeks were wet with tears. "Are you sure you want to say anymore?"

Sara nodded. "It's important." She dabbed her face with a napkin and took a sip of water. "Anyway, they headed off. I waved from the back porch as they disappeared into the woods, my last glimpse of my two beautiful stepchildren. I fell asleep in my chair and awoke an hour or so later as Whip ran into the yard shrieking. Poor thing was delirious. He clawed at me, screaming, 'Puma, puma, puma! Help!'

"I called John, and he and two of his men were in the yard in ATVs within what seemed like seconds. Whip was crumpled in my lap sobbing, but when he saw his dad, he jumped up and begged to go with them. John should have refused. We knew that at the time, but there was always the chance that they'd diverged from the main path and John might need Whip to show them the way. He took him up on his lap and sped off. All three of the men were armed. What they found was something no father should see, much less a child.

"Both Ellie and Johnny were dead, mauled and almost unrecognizable. One of the cougars was still there, attempting to drag Johnny's body into the thick woods. They shot her and they wounded her mate, who was standing over Ellie.

"When they returned, our poor children's bodies were strapped to the ATVs, nothing to cover the terrible carnage. Whip was comatose, eyes glazed and trembling violently. As I scooped him into my arms, my water broke. They called the ambulance and took us both to West

Coast General Hospital, where Addie was delivered two hours later, Whip still locked in my arms. I don't know how we did it, any of us. My husband was devastated. I blamed myself and would have locked myself in my room had I not had my two babies to care for."

"Oh Sara, I am so sorry." Bella reached forward and hugged her.

"Thank goodness for sweet little Addie. Whip adored her, and she gave us all something to live for, a source of joy and smiles amid the wreckage."

Bella held her for several minutes, then Sara gave her a squeeze and pulled back. A wan smile played across her handsome face even as her eyes reflected unfathomable sadness. "Whip went through hell. We've watched helpless as he fell apart, unable to speak, rocking for hours, lost in his own world. It wasn't until he finally pulled things together that we could all go on. He saw a child psychologist for a few years. She was helpful in getting him through the worst, helping him to speak again. Then when he was eight and a half, he announced, 'No more shrinks,' and refused to go anymore. He's remained resolute until this past week.

"In the past, the minute he got close to someone, he'd break it off. As I said, he worshiped his older siblings, and I think he's scared to death to get close to someone for fear of losing them. Then he met you. Something's different this time. We all see it. Even if my husband keeps telling me to leave it alone, he senses it too. Something's motivating our son to do the work of healing. I believe that something or someone is you, Bella. He wants to get better for you. I wanted to tell you all this in case you're willing to be patient with him?"

"Of course," Bella said, placing a hand over Sara's. "I'm in love with your son. Of course, I can and will be patient."

Sara smiled. "I thought so! Women's intuition is seldom wrong."

"Is there anything you think I can do to help support him?"

"I think you're doing all the right things, my dear. Now let's finish our sandwiches and get you back to work."

"Have you got a way back to Morgan's Run?"

"Yes, I have the SUV. Ben Morgan drove John and Addie up to the farm. I understand it's lovely, but this was more important to me," she said. "Thank you for making time."

After leaving Sara at her car, Bella walked back to the office, stunned by the other's revelations. *Whatever happens, I'll be by his side if he lets me, and even if he doesn't,* she thought, pushing open the door of Valley Ob-Gyn.

CHAPTER 24

Ben Senior, Spark, and Harley came down to see one more training session with Ghost. As Whip led him through his paces, the stallion was alternately obstinate and almost docile, but it was clear they'd made up their minds. "Have you gotten a saddle on him?" Harley called.

"Not yet, but we're getting there," Tom said. "He tolerates a blanket sometimes."

"How 'bout today?" Ben asked.

Whip shook his head.

"Let's give it a try and see how he does," Harley said. "Tom, what do you think?"

"I defer to Whip. He knows him best. The horse is much calmer now that Patty's treating his mouth issues."

"Whaddya say, son?" Ben called. "Can you try the blanket?"

Whip wanted to protest. Ghost was doing okay, but he sensed something was upsetting him with all the snorting and erratic behavior. *But if I refuse, that'll be worse*, he thought, heading for the fence where several blankets hung. He slung a light one over his shoulder and began running the stallion around the round pen, the lead loose as he changed directions every loop or two. "That a boy," he said softly as Ghost responded to his every signal.

Finally, he paused and turned his back on the horse, slowly walking away, letting Ghost come to him. "Good boy," he said, voice soft as the horse nudged his shoulder.

Spark chuckled. "Looks like he's telling him a secret. He's come a long way with him, hasn't he?"

Tom nodded just as Whip turned and walked to the stallion's side, patting his withers, then moving to the curve of his back. "Good boy, good boy," he continued, holding the blanket near Ghost's nose, rubbing it along his shoulder until finally, he slipped it over his back. "Good boy," he said, just as Ghost turned and reared up, emitting a loud, angry whinny, hooves flailing out in front of him.

"Step away!" Tom called, but Whip stood his ground.

"It's okay, boy," he said, his eyes following the hooves' movements, standing clear. The blanket had slipped off Ghost's back and lay in the dust. It now seemed to be the object of Ghost's tantrum, and his hooves continued to rain down on it, burying it in the dirt.

"The little stinker," Harley said to Tom as they watched horse and man. "Kittredge, time to get the hell out of there. Now."

Reluctantly, Whip dropped the lead and headed for the fence as Ghost continued his attack on the blanket. "Yesterday, he did great with it. He's spooked today for some reason. I heard two hikers encountered a mountain lion yesterday, so they're still around. Ghost notices everything, and he still considers himself leader of his herd. That's why he and Dusty don't get along," he said. "It's getting better, though."

Ben nodded. "I know about the cougars. Maggie has had to shut down all trail riding this week after one was spotted in the north pasture. Bottom line is, one of them has to go—Ghost or Dusty. The Kiger's more valuable to us. I'm sorry, son. There's a truck coming through Monday, and Ghost has a place on it."

"You're going to send him to slaughter, then?" Whip cried, more desperately than he intended.

"Not necessarily. They'll take him to auction. There's always the chance that someone'll want a challenge. He's a beautiful horse, so you never know."

"I know," Whip said, jumping the fence. "If you'll excuse me, I'll get back to work. I'll be back in a couple of hours to put him in."

"I'm sorry, Tom," Ben said. "I know he's heartbroken, but it's just too risky."

"He knows that," Tom said. "It's my fault. I let him get too close to Ghost. Let him off work to spend all this time with him. Let him bond with a horse that's not his own. He'll be fine once Ghost heads out and he gets back into his usual work routines."

A DISTRAUGHT, angry Whip stomped up the road to the stables. The stalls were cleaned, but several of the horses needed exercise, so he volunteered, taking one, then the next one out for fifteen-minute intervals on the track. As he came in on one, Greg brought the next out, saddled and ready, while leading the previous horse back into the stables to remove the tack and brush him or her down. During one of these hand-offs, he said, "You okay, man?"

"No, but I'm just a lowly ranch hand, and no one gives a shit about what I think."

"So, they're still giving Ghost the heave-ho, then?"

"Don't want to talk about it," Whip said, mounting Blue, the tall gray Trakehner. The massive animal towered over both men at eighteen hands, but was always gentle and calm.

As he rounded the track for the final loop with Blue, Whip spied Bella's SUV coming down the drive and waved. She pulled over and slid out, coming to stand by the fence. "Hi!"

Whip guided Blue toward her. "Hey."

"No Ghost today?" she asked, smiling up at him. Bella could tell he was upset by the set of his shoulders, his handsome face creased in a frown.

"He's just been given his death sentence, so what's the point?"

"What about his treatments?" she asked, wanting to hop the fence and throw her arms around him. That is, if he wasn't sitting on a horse almost as tall and substantial as a Clydesdale.

Whip shrugged. "Doesn't matter. They think he's too much of a risk, and they're right. I'll just hate to see him go."

"I'm sorry. Did your parents get off okay?"

He nodded. "One last lunch at Gracie's and off they went. They're in Sedona for a couple of days now, talking to Robbie's old partners, then home."

"You around tonight?"

"Nope. We've got a planning meeting at Harley's for Saturday's event."

"Well, I guess I'll see you around. I'm only working a half day tomorrow so I can meet Grace and Ruthie in the afternoon. Ruthie took a day off and wants to bring the kids to see the mustangs. Plus, Grace is going to show us all of Dusty's new tricks."

"Okay, then," he said, as he turned Blue away toward the track. "I should probably get old Blue back and grab my next victim."

"Whip?" she called, reluctant to let him go. "Are you okay?"

"Nope, but I'll survive. I'd suggest skipping your evening walk tonight. More cougar sightings, and they're close by."

"I hope they move back to higher ground soon."

"Who knows? They've found food down here, and they're feeding cubs. From what I hear, all the ranches are doing what we're doing, stocking up on bear and pepper spray. We have cartons of both in the barn behind the stables."

"I have a couple of cans," she said.

"Good. Much better than that shotgun you've been toting around. If a cougar came after you, you wouldn't have time to use it, but you might get off a shot of pepper spray. They hate it."

"Thanks for the tip. When will I see you?"

He smiled. "Probably tomorrow when the kids come. I'll be with Ghost, and they always like to watch that."

She wanted to say more, much more, but she could sense him shutting down and pulling away, so she simply said, "Okay. See ya." Her heart ached as he and Blue galloped off, man and horse in perfect sync.

CHAPTER 25

"What do you think?" Whip asked, eyes trained on Haley's. "Have I made any progress or am I hopeless?"

The therapist smiled. "Only you can say if you've made progress. That's an internal understanding. I don't think you're hopeless. It sounds as if you love Bella very much, so I suggest that a next step would be to share with her. Let her in, let her see the whole man you are, a man with a painful past who wants his future to be with her."

WHIP and the crew completed their work at the stables, and he and Greg grabbed sandwiches from the lunch spread Fran, the ranch cook, had set out for them. As they strolled down to the barn, Greg asked, "So, you working with Ghost this afternoon?"

Whip nodded. "Ruthie's bringing the kids. They love watching him."

Greg chuckled. "They love watching their cowboy hero, you mean."

Whip gave him a look. "Grace is coming to work with Dusty too."

"Cameras caught a cougar ten feet from stables last night, did you hear?" Greg asked, referring to the security cameras recently installed behind the thoroughbred stables. "One of the guards scared him off."

"I heard. When the hell are they gonna get cameras down here?" Whip muttered as they walked through the clean, empty barn, the scent of freshly laid hay almost intoxicating. "The guys did good work in here this morning."

"Always do, especially when we know the boss's wife's paying a visit."

"You know Ruthie won't even notice," Whip said. He grabbed the shotgun and headed on through and up to the paddocks.

"But her dad might," Greg said, following him. "You take that up every day now?"

"Only when I'm there and kids are coming," Whip answered, already halfway up to the large round pen where Ghost stood waiting. Greg followed him and would deal with the other horses, the new mustangs, and the others, scattered in three other large corrals in case the kids wanted to see them. They'd also saddled Pokey, a short stocky pinto, the gentlest of the barn horses, in case Charlotte wanted a ride. Greg would help with that too.

Shortly after the two men reached the corrals, Bella and Grace appeared. "Hey, ladies," Greg called. Whip tipped his hat, but directed his attention to Ghost. The minute he stepped into the round pen, he sensed the stallion's extreme agitation. Ghost paced, snorted, and stamped his hooves, his breathing heavy and thick.

Bella also recognized something was off. She called good luck to Grace, then came to the edge of Ghost's enclosure. "He seems unsettled," she said softly.

"That's an understatement. Where's your brother?"

"With Harley. They're meeting with some suppliers, I think. Why?"

"Just wish he was here. Doesn't seem like the best day for the kids to come. No telling what he'll do. I don't have the authority to say no to Ruthie Langdon, but he does."

"Of course, you have the authority if you think it's dangerous."

"Not dangerous, but he's so riled up, I doubt he'll be very coop-erative."

"Then leave him be. The kids don't need a show. They're coming for a picnic, a quick peek at all the pretty horses, and maybe a pony ride. Give Ghost the day off," Bella said as her eyes came to rest on the shotgun hanging out of reach inside the fence.

"Yeah, probably best," he said, unhooking Ghost's long lead. He patted him gently, then headed for the fence. The stallion followed him, resting his head on Whip's shoulder. Whip smiled, looked up at her, then reached around to pet the huge horse. "Good boy," he said, softly, patting his nose and leaning to rest his face against Ghost's shoulder. After thirty seconds of fussing, the stallion snorted and pulled back, trotting to the opposite side of the pen.

Whip grinned. "He's not much for mushiness." He jumped the fence in one fluid motion and landed near her.

He has no idea how gorgeous he is, Bella mused, her body warm and tingly as she recalled their crazy lovemaking behind the barn at Harley and Ruthie's.

"Here they come." Whip gazed over her shoulder toward the barn. Ruthie and Willow emerged from the shadows. Ruthie held a large picnic basket and Charlotte's hand, while Willow had Pickles on her hip.

Ruthie hiked up the basket so her hand was free to wave. "Got enough food here for an army!"

"Figures, we just ate at the bunkhouses," Whip said to Bella. "That basket probably came from the Big House. Fran's good, but she's no Carmela.

Bella laughed as they walked down to meet the four. "I'm sure you can squeeze in a little more."

"Carmela does make the best cookies in the world," he said. As he passed by the other enclosures, he called to Grace and Greg to take a break and come have something to eat. Blankets were spread on a level stretch of freshly mowed grass. They all relaxed as Charlotte ran back and forth along the fence lines. She knew all the horses by name, and most came over to greet her, even Ghost.

As they observed Ghost bending his head, allowing the beautiful child with her mother's light red curls to pet his nose, Bella said, "He may be an ornery old guy, but he sure loves her, doesn't he?" As she turned back, she spied Charlotte's grandfather and Harley headed their way.

"Hey, Dad!" Ruthie called.

"Papa!" Charlotte cried, running down the hill and into first her father's arms, then her grandfather's.

"Taking a break to come see my granddaughters," Ben said. He took a seat on the blanket, kissing his youngest child. "Hey, sweetie. Don't you look pretty." And she did. Ruthie Morgan Langdon looked great in overalls, ball gowns, and everything in between. Today, she wore denim capris and a blousy white top that made breast-feeding easy. She'd kicked off her sandals and was barefoot. Harley kissed the top of her head. "Hey, babe."

The group chatted as Harley took his daughter in for a ride on Pokey. Whip stood at the fence, watching father and daughter, his gaze constantly moving from one enclosure to the other. He'd picked up on Ghost's agitation and couldn't settle down himself.

As Ruthie watched Charlotte, she let out a big sigh. "She loves Pokey, and we've promised her a pony when she turns four, but she's really going to miss Ghost. Dad, are you and Spark sure about him? Where is Spark today anyway?"

Bella observed Ben Senior's kind blue eyes as they moved from his daughter to Charlotte, in heaven on horseback, her adoring father at her side. "You know I'd do anything for my grandchildren, but this is a safety issue for the stables. He's a magnificent animal, but he's too risky."

Ruthie sighed. "I know."

"Where will you keep Charlotte's pony?" Bella asked, deciding that a change of subject was in order.

"Our house. We already have my horse, Jadie, and Pepper, Harley's huge brute. We have plenty of room for one little pony in the barn."

"I'm surprised Harley doesn't ride to work every day. It's not that far, is it?"

"'Bout five miles by the Loop Trail. He does once in a while. Poor Pepper loves to run, and he's getting fat with too little exercise. I've been begging him to bring Pep down to the stables and have the guys exercise him, but Harley says no one else can handle him."

"Not far from the truth," her father said. "There are some one-man horses, and that ole Appaloosa is one of 'em. That's my opinion, anyway. If you're busy and want to bring Jadie down here or over to the ranch, I'm pretty sure she'd get lots of attention."

"Unlike my husband, I ride every day after work before I pick up the kids, but now that you mention it, I've been considering bringing her to the ranch if Maggie has room. Much more convenient. With the kids at the Cottage, I can ride after or before work."

Conversation drifted off, and Charlotte returned, begging for another cookie. Harley, Tom, and Whip stood talking by the fence as Greg walked among the horses in the main corral. Grace stood up and announced she would spend a little time with Dusty. She headed toward his corral, leaving Ben Senior, Ruthie, Willow, and Bella on the blanket. Pickles was asleep in her stroller nearby.

"I'm gonna go pick flowers Mommy," Charlotte announced, her half-eaten cookie dangling in her hand as she skipped off toward the open field just north of the paddocks.

Ruthie blew her a kiss. "Okay, but don't go too far, baby."

The group settled back, chatting in the languid stillness of the afternoon. Usually green and moist, the Valley was in the midst of a heat wave. Today, the air was heavy with moisture, and thunderstorms were predicted for the evening hours. Charlotte was gathering wildflowers, a hundred yards beyond the outmost corral, when her mother screamed, "Harley!" just as a blood-chilling sound came from Ghost's pen.

As Bella gazed in horror, a tawny creature moved swiftly across the meadow, closing in on the oblivious child. Whip grabbed the gun as Harley and Tom began running full tilt toward Charlotte. Even so, it was clear they wouldn't reach her before the cougar. Then, without a sound, a white streak cleared the round pen fence and raced across the field. Ghost reached the cougar now five feet from the child and reared up, his hooves crashing down on the snarling creature again and again.

As the horse continued his assault, Harley scooped up his daughter and ran for Dusty's corral. As father and daughter scaled the fence, the others crowded in except Whip, who continued to walk slowly and steadily toward Ghost, who had clearly killed the mountain lion. Bella realized as she watched, her brother beside her, that Whip's attention was not on the horse, but beyond, where the cougar's mate stood ready to strike. As she moved, he raised the shotgun and fired. The animal dropped instantly.

"That was quite a shot," Ben Senior said, his arm around Willow, who trembled at his side. In the other arm, he cradled his baby granddaughter, who was still asleep.

Whip put his hand up toward Ghost, "It's over boy," he said. "Good boy."

He expected the horse to follow, but instead, the stallion reared up once, whinnying in triumph, then galloped toward the corrals, ignoring the round pen and easily clearing the fence of the main paddock, where all the other mustangs, except Dusty, grazed. Once inside, he stood, calm and majestic. Home with his herd at last.

"Jeez," Greg said, giving voice to all of their thoughts. "Guess you got a jumper in case the stables ever want to have a show-jumping program."

Tom shook his head. "I've never seen anything like it. Is she okay?" he asked, turning to Ruthie and Harley, who held Charlotte.

"She's fine, aren't you, baby?" Ruthie said. Bella noticed that both parents' cheeks were wet with tears.

"Ghostie saved me, Papa," Charlotte said to her grandfather. "You can't send him away now, can you?"

Ben Senior walked over and hugged the three of them. "No, we can't, baby girl. Ghostie's staying with us, no matter what."

As she observed from a distance, Bella realized her cheeks too were wet. She brushed away the tears and slipped out of Tom's grasp to climb the fence. She walked toward Whip, who stood over the trampled cougar.

"Bad idea," Harley said.

Tom called, "Wait, Bella, it might not be safe."

Ignoring them, she quickened her pace as she neared the man she loved more than life itself.

"Hey," she said softly, placing a hand on his shoulder. He looked up, a dazed expression on his handsome face. For a second, it looked like he didn't recognize her. Then Bella opened her arms, and he straightened up.

"It's over," he said quietly as he pulled her into his strong arms. "It's over."

"Yes, my love. It's over."

Only when Tom and Harley reached them did they break apart.

"Good job, buddy," Tom said, patting Whip's shoulder.

"Are they both dead?" Harley asked.

Whip nodded. "Male and female. Probably hunting for their cubs. We'll have to send a party out to try to locate them. They won't survive on their own."

"Leave 'em for now. I'll organize that when we get back," Harley said. "We can call the rangers. They'll assist with the search and cleanup."

The four walked back to the picnic site, now packed up. Ruthie, Willow, and the children had already started toward the car, Ben Senior with them. Harley waved, then headed for drive to help load the children into their new Rover. They'd purchased the vehicle before Pickles's birth to replace Ruthie's antique green truck, which was now parked in their barn.

Grace and Tom stood together talking as Bella and Whip observed the reunited herd. "Whaddya think, boss?" Greg asked, not clear if he was addressing Tom or Whip. "Should we leave Ghost where he is or try to separate them?"

Tom chuckled. "Well, as we just witnessed, Ghost goes wherever he wants, so what's the point? I think you should observe them, though, till we bring 'em in just in case intervention is required."

"Sure thing." Greg stole a glance at Whip.

Tom turned to Whip. "You take the rest of the day off, buddy."

His assistant handed him the shotgun. "No way boss. I'm staying with Ghost. He may be hurt. Can we see if Patty can come down and take a look?"

"I'll call her," Tom said, looking over at his sister before turning away.

"I'll stay too," she said quietly.

CHAPTER 26

"Minor scratches," Patty Turner said after examining Ghost. The stallion was remarkably calm as the vet stood beside Whip, running her hands along the horse's back and legs. "Just to be sure, I'm recommending he have the rabies series. We have the meds in stock, but I'll need permission from one of the owners or Harley. Once I get that, I'll come back down." She turned to Whip. "I'll need you to be with me. Is that a problem?"

"No. I plan to stay with him, so I'll be here."

"I'll text or call when I'm on my way," Patty said, closing her bag and stepping out of the stall. "See you later." She nodded to Bella, who had been watching from the other side of the gate.

Whip stood, resting his head on the horse's back for several minutes, then with one last "Good boy," he stepped out of the corral and closed the gate. Bella followed him to the bench just outside the barn where he sat, head between his legs, and sobbed. She sat beside him, arm over his shoulder, patting his back. After a few minutes, he looked up, meeting her eyes. "Pretty pathetic, huh?"

"No," she said, stroking his cheek with her fingertips. "Would you like me to get you some dinner? I could drive into town or see If I can get something delivered."

"I'm fine, thanks. I'm sure Fran has leftovers up at the bunkhouse kitchen. Greg'll save me some, or I can scrounge around in the fridge. Besides, I'd like to tell you something, if you don't have to run off."

Bella smiled. "I'm here as long as you need me. All night if necessary."

"My mom told me she spoke to you before they left. About Ellie and Johnny."

"Yes."

"What she didn't tell you, because I've never spoken about it, was what happened that day. I gave Haley a summary, but even she doesn't know all of it."

Bella placed her hands over his. "I'm here."

Whip gulped, his hands shaking as he turned to her. "It was a great morning, sunny and hot. We were so happy hiking in the woods. Lots of shade. We were about halfway to Lizard Pond when it happened. We were excited to climb down to the beach and swim. Much cooler than taking the road. My mom would have been with us, and she did offer to drive us. There's a dirt road that leads into the pond, but we wanted to hike, to have a cool adventure. We were all good swimmers and there's a lifeguard at the pond. Plus she trusted Johnny and Ellie to look after me. They were really responsible.

"Johnny was in the lead, then me, then Ellie. We'd just stepped into a clearing when I heard Ellie scream, then a thud right behind me. When I turned, the cougar had her by the throat. I'm pretty sure she died quickly. Before I could go to her, Johnny grabbed a hold of me and threw me off the trail into the brush.

"'Run, Whip, run!' he yelled, but a second cougar had stepped into the clearing. Just like today, they were hunting together, which actually is kind of unusual for mountain lions. From what I know, they usually stalk their prey alone. I hesitated, and he yelled again, just as the second cougar jumped on him. I didn't want to go, but I fought my way through the brush and did as he told me. When I passed Ellie's body, the cougar was already ripping at the flesh on her shoulder."

Bella struggled with waves of nausea at the image, but said nothing as she held his hands tightly.

"I ran the whole way, almost bust my lungs. When I came into the backyard, I started screaming like hell, and my mom came out on the back porch. I was panting so hard, it took me a few minutes to tell her what had happened. She told me to go get the cart while she ran into the house to call my dad.

"In those days we kept an old golf cart that my mom used mostly for gardening. Ordinarily I wasn't allowed to drive it unless my dad was with me. By the time I'd driven around from the barn, he'd raced in. He had two other guys with him in ATVs. He insisted that my mom stay home. She was in pain, holding her stomach. He didn't want to take me, but he needed to be sure we followed the right path. While we set off, my mom ran in the house to call the rangers.

"When we got to the clearing, my sister's face was gone, and the cougars were dragging Johnny off. One of his arms was detached from his body. They'd gotten him in the neck too. There was blood everywhere. The last thing I remember are gunshots and my father's rage. 'Bastards, bastards, bastards!' he kept yelling. Then my brain shut down.

"They tell me I didn't talk for almost a year. I have no recollection of anything after the sound of my dad's gun. In fact, I don't recall anything clearly till I was in third grade. I guess they sent me to school, but I just sat there. Said nothing, didn't interact with anyone. Nothing. Until I started up with Haley last week, I've never spoken about the attack to anyone. Not my parents, teachers, or the long line of child psychologists they took me to."

By the time he finished talking, it was dark, and the stars were shining in a moonless sky. "Oh Whip, I am so sorry," Bella said, wrapping her arms around him, knowing that no words could ever take away the horror.

Suddenly he reached in his pocket and pulled out his cell phone. "That's Patty. She's on her way."

They walked arm and arm into the barn and waited for the vet. She gave Ghost the first rabies shot, said good night, and left them alone.

"Thanks," he said, squeezing Bella's hand. "I'm going to stay with Ghost, but you should head home and get some sleep."

"If you don't mind, I'll sit with you for a while," she said as he dragged several hay bales to the floor just outside Ghost's stall.

"I'd usually sleep in the stall if a horse is sick, but with Ghost, better to be safe."

They sat down beside each other, his arm around her, Bella's head on his chest. It felt so good to feel his warmth against her cheek that she closed her eyes. "I love you," she whispered, unsure whether he heard her or was already asleep. An occasional howl of a coyote, nickering from the stalls, or the cry of a night hawk in the distance lulled them to sleep.

CHAPTER 27

Bella woke before sunrise and brushed hay from her jeans. Whip was already awake, standing watching over Ghost. "Morning," she said, standing up. "How is he?"

"Good."

"And you?"

"Body's felt better, but otherwise, I'm good too." He pulled her into his arms. "Did you tell me you loved me last night?" he asked trailing kisses down her neck.

"Yes," she said, looking up to give him a shy smile.

"And did I say I love you back?"

"Not that I heard."

"Well, I'll say it now. then—I love you. Then all's right in my world." He kissed her softly. "Only one problem."

"What's that?"

"The crew'll be here any minute, so no time to drag you up to the loft."

Bella smiled, her fingers playing along his strong jaw. "I've got to go to work anyway."

"So, we'll get together soon?" he asked as the sounds of men's voices drew nearer.

"I'd like that."

"I'll think of something."

"Good. I'm going to duck out the back." Bella kissed him one more time.

"You won't fool anyone, you know," he said, chuckling.

"At least I don't have to speak to anyone. Have a great day."

"You too. I love you, Bella."

"I love you too," she said, then she pulled away from his warmth and hurried out the back door of the barn.

AT HOME, she tiptoed upstairs to shower. When she came down, Tom had breakfast prepared. "Morning." He set a plate of scrambled eggs, bacon, and hash browns in front of her. "I packed your lunch too. It's in the fridge."

Bella poured herself a large mug of coffee and sat down. "Well, this is a surprise. I'd have thought you'd be gone by now."

"Had to make sure you had sustenance after your night in the hay."

"Thanks. Truth be told, I am a little stiff. So, my tiptoeing earlier didn't fool you?"

Her brother took the last bite of his breakfast, a grin on his face. "I came down to check on things at around midnight. Found you two curled up in the hay. Wish I'd had my phone to take a picture."

"Ha-ha."

"No, I'm serious. You looked real cute."

"Well, we will not be repeating it for a photo op. Are you upset?"

"Nope."

"He's been through hell."

"Yup, I always figured there was something."

"I love him, Tom."

"I know, and he's crazy about you."

"You don't object?"

"You're a thirty-two-year-old woman. Would it really matter if I did?"

"Only because it's important to me that you like him."

Tom laughed. "I like him well enough. Hell, if I didn't like him, he wouldn't be working here and I wouldn't ask him to watch out for my sister on her idiotic evening walks, would I? Talk about throwing two people together."

"I love you, big brother," she said, reaching across the table to take his hand.

"Right back at you, sis. Now, I've gotta get to work. You okay?"

"Great. This is delicious, by the way. Thanks. I'll clean up."

Bella couldn't stop smiling as she stacked dishes in the dishwasher and scrubbed the cast iron skillet. She might be bone-tired, but as Whip said, all was right with her world too.

EVENTS at the stables kept the crew busy all weekend. Saturday, there was also the work of burying the cougar carcasses. Vultures circled the area as the men worked alongside the rangers, digging holes deep enough that the carrion wouldn't be dug up. Bella went into the office as she was the on-call midwife, and it was easier to be there than at home if she got called to a birth.

She ate dinner in town that night with Tom and Grace. When she and her brother got home, she laced up her sneakers and donned her head lamp. "You've gotta be kidding," Tom said, observing her. "After all that's happened, you're actually going out? It's dark."

"I'll stick to the track. Besides, maybe the pair that were killed were the only cougars around."

"If you believe that, you're an idiot."

"Thanks a lot."

"I mean it, Bella. The warnings are still up. Unless you get Whip or one of the guys to go with you, I can't let you go."

She smiled. "Fine. I'll call him."

"Nice move," he said.

Whip agreed to meet her in fifteen minutes, but when she stepped out a few minutes later, he was sitting on the porch steps. "Evenin'."

"Hi," she said. "Did Tom text and tell you to come down?"

He grinned, the porch light illuminating his handsome, craggy features. "Nope. I thought this one up all by myself."

"Aren't you a smart one," she said.

She took his hand as they strolled toward the drive, then Whip put his arm around her and kissed her temple. "I missed you today."

"Me too, you," she said, resting her head against him. "You okay?"

"Tired, but I'm gonna be...okay, I mean. Or I hope."

"I'm glad... Tired too. We both need a good night's sleep. How did Ghost do today?"

"Total transformation. We let him in with the others, and he was calm, no skirmishes, even with Dusty. The two are keeping their distance, but it almost seems like they've made an equine truce."

She stopped and looked over at him. "Is that a real thing?"

Whip laughed. "No, but none of this seems real, to tell you the truth. Walking here with you, the cougars, everything."

They rounded the track in the starry night, the usual country sounds punctuating the quiet. As they reached the bunkhouses, she turned to him, her arms circling his shoulders. "Thanks, I can make it from here."

In answer, his lips found hers, and they were instantly lost in a breathless embrace. When he broke the kiss, he whispered, "I'm walking you home, although I'd love to sneak you into my bunkhouse and tear your clothes off."

Bella smiled, kissing him lightly. "Sounds amazing. We'll save that for another night."

"Yup."

"Night, my love."

"You forget, I'm walking you home."

"Aren't I the lucky woman?"

After saying good night to Whip, Bella stepped into the house and found Tom on the sofa, waiting. "We just walked," she said, wondering if she was about to get a lecture.

"Not about that... I mean good. Walking is good, but this is something different."

Bella took a seat beside him on the sofa, fearing the worst. "What is it?"

"Dad's had a heart attack. It was a mild one, but Mom's a basket case and is asking for one of us to fly to Naples."

"I'll go. That's the best solution. They can't spare you, and after this past crazy weekend, I don't have any patients about to give birth. They can cover me better than you."

"Are you sure?"

"Positive. I'll phone Mark in the morning. When is Mom expecting me?"

"Tomorrow."

"What?"

"I called Harley a few minutes ago to tell him, and he was having dinner at Spark's with the Morgans. After we hung up, he called back to say that Spark will have the jet fueled and ready to go first thing or whenever you're ready."

"Can we accept that?"

"I don't see how we can refuse. He's got his pilot, Mickey Collins, standing by."

"That quick?" she asked, incredulous.

"That's how billionaires do it. Just lucky Mickey was in town, but if he wasn't, I'm guessing that Spark could have had him here at Grenville Airport by noon."

"What time should we tell him?"

"Spark's suggesting ten, so that way, you'll arrive by dinner."

Bella shook her head. "Well, I'd better get packing. It's too late to call Mark tonight, but I was planning to take Monday and Tuesday off anyway, so I'll phone on the way to the airport. I'm sure it'll be fine."

"Are you sure?" Tom asked.

His sister nodded. "Call Spark and see if ten will work for Mickey.

Ask him what time I need to be at the airport too. Oh, gee, how am I going to get there?"

"Spark offered to send a car, but I'll work something out and also call Mom. She'll be relieved. You go pack."

Life turns on a dime, she thought as she headed upstairs.

CHAPTER 28

It was just after seven when brother and sister hugged alongside Whip's truck. "Take care, sis," Tom said. Whip stowed her suitcase in the back of the truck. "Drive carefully," he said to his assistant, "and you have a safe flight."

"I'll try," she said. "This whole thing is so surreal, I don't know what to think."

"Enjoy, is my advice. I hear the jet's pretty amazing."

And off they went.

On the forty-five-minute drive to Grenville Airport, Whip said, "Sure was a surprise to get Tom's call."

"Surprise that he asked you to drive me, or what's happened, or where I'm going?"

"All of the above. You never talk about your parents."

"Not much to say. I'll have more info when I return."

"When will that be?"

"I'll know more when I get there. I'm guessing one or two weeks, during which time I will miss you every minute of every day."

He smiled. "Not every second?"

"That too, every second!" Bella reached over and stroked his arm.

"I'll miss you too," he said. "More than you'll ever know.

A CAR WAITED at the Naples airport and transported Bella straight to the hospital. When she asked the driver who had ordered the service, he said, "Ms. Jacobi. Her message was: Have my daughter come straight to the hospital. I need her."

Bella leaned back and closed her eyes. She'd napped several times on the flight east. The seats in Spark's plane fully reclined, and the attendant, a lovely woman named Janice, had furnished her with a light down comforter. Even after four-plus hours in the lap of luxury, she was still tired. The emotional roller coaster of the past few weeks had been exhausting. Even though she would rather be in Saguaro, maybe a short vacation was just what she needed.

As they pulled into the hospital parking lot, she asked the driver to wait while she sent two texts, one to Tom, the other to Whip, letting them know she'd arrived safely. *Now for Mother*, she thought, wondering what she'd find inside. The driver brought her suitcase around, and she thanked him. The driver refused a tip, and they parted company. *Fortunately, I travel light*, she mused as she pulled her small suitcase into hospital lobby.

When she emerged from the elevator on the cardiac floor, she had no difficulty locating her father's room since her mother's voice carried all the way down the long hall. When she peeked in the door, the bed was empty, and Angela Jacobi was berating a CNA for the way she was remaking the bed. "And what kind of pillows are these?" she demanded, holding up a thin rubber pillow waiting for its case. "Is this a prison or a hospital?"

Bella shoved her suitcase in a corner and came forward, reading the nametag on the CNA's chest. "Hey, Mother, let's let Ramona do her job. Where's Dad?"

"Oh Bella! Thank God you're here," she said, hugging her daughter.

"Why don't we find something to drink?" She guided her mother out of the room.

There was a lounge just down the hall with vending machines.

Mercifully, it was vacant, so she pushed her mother toward a seat. "Sit. I'll get us some tea."

Obediently Angela sat, her lime-green golf skirt rumpled, matching floral top askew. A pretty woman, her shoulder length silver hair was stylishly coiffed, albeit a bit ruffled at present. *A new look for Mom*, Bella thought as she brought the tea and sat beside her on the Naugahyde sofa. "So, what's going on Mom? Where's Dad?"

Her mother waved her hand. "Down having some test or other. They say the attack was mild and they gave him meds to thin his blood and dissolve any clots. They're running blood tests to check for some kinds of heart proteins. Cardiac markers, the doctor said. They want to keep him for two or three days. I can't believe it," she said, gazing over at Bella, her eyes wild.

"What happened?"

"He just slumped over at the breakfast table. Didn't say anything, just landed in his poached eggs."

"Well, it's good that it's mild, right?"

"They won't know the full story till they do more tests. I think they're doing a cardiac CT tomorrow."

"And how are you holding up?" Bella asked, her arm circling her mother's shoulders.

"Not well, as you could see with my tantrum at the poor nurse."

"She's a CNA and I'm sure she's heard it all before. You can apologize later. Now, what time did they say Dad would be back?"

"Soon, which is why I called for the bed to be changed. My poor Tommy. He's so been enjoying his retirement—golf, tennis, new friends, and all."

"And he still will. Exercise is encouraged after a heart episode. Now let's go wait in his room. I'm sure Ramona's got his bed all set."

Tom Jacobi Senior was wheeled in twenty minutes later. His color was good, but he looked exhausted.

"Hey, Dad," she said as the gurney passed by.

"Bella! Honey, what are you doing here?" Her father was a robust man with ruddy cheeks and a Leprechaun's smile. She noticed that his broad shoulders strained the seams of his johnny and made a mental note to ask if they had a larger size later.

"You get settled and then we'll talk," she said as the orderlies transferred him from gurney to bed and tucked him in.

After hugging him, Bella sat beside the bed, holding his hand. Her mother had collapsed in a recliner nearby. "I had to come east to check on you. Plus, how could I turn down an invitation to Naples? Tom told me to take lots of pictures."

"How'd you get here so quickly, baby?"

She smiled. "It pays to know billionaires with private jets. One of Tom's bosses lent it to me."

"Ranching must pay good out there."

"Spark made his money in alternative energy. Still does. Ranching is his hobby with his best friend, Ben Morgan. They own the thoroughbred farm where Tom works and we live. You should see the house they gave him. You'll have to come visit."

"So good to see you, sweetie." He squeezed her hand as he closed his eyes. Bella turned to see why her mother had been so quiet and found her now asleep in her recliner.

BELLA HAD SEEN pictures of the Naples house, but still wasn't prepared for its size or grandeur. Her mother called it French West-Indies style. The home's three wings surrounded an enormous pool, koi ponds, and lush gardens. The interior's soaring ceilings and tasteful furnishings, in a palette of whites, beiges, and soft pastels, were awe-inspiring. Bella listened, incredulous, as her mother talked about their decorator. Their Montana home had been comfortable and handsome, but nothing like this palace on the bay.

The two weeks in Naples flew by in a flurry of activity, from getting her father home, arranging for nursing visits, grocery shopping, and driving her mother here and there. One morning toward the end of her stay, Angela announced at breakfast, "I'm taking you shopping this afternoon. Judging by the clothes you brought, you've let your wardrobe go."

Realizing that protest would fall on deaf ears, Bella agreed. "As long as you'll be okay, Dad?" They hadn't left him alone since they'd brought him home.

"By all means, go! You girls have fun, and I can enjoy some peace and quiet without any mother hens hovering around."

Bella lost count of the number of shops and boutiques they visited, but came home at the end of the day with bags of tops, slacks, capris, and a few skirts and dresses. She predicted she'd never wear half of it, but the excursion made her mother happy."

When it was time to say goodbye, she found herself both wistful about leaving and eager to get home. They'd ordered her a car and she'd booked a commercial flight, which her mother insisted on upgrading to first class. "Got to keep up with your Mr. Spark," she said.

Bella hugged her dad one last time, then her mother. "It's been great to see you both," she said, and meant it. "I hope we can get you out to the Valley sometime soon. You'll love it. Maybe Mr. Spark would even offer the jet?"

"Once your dad's on his feet, we'll make a plan. And of course, we'll come for your brother's wedding, whenever that will be," Angela said, as mother and daughter walked out to the front drive. "Thank you so much for coming, honey. It meant the world to your dad and me."

Bella glimpsed tears in her mother's eyes and gave her a last hug. "He's going to be fine, Mom. You heard the doctors. He's strong as an ox, his heart too."

"Oh doctors, what do they know? It was just scary, that's all. He's the love of my life and my best friend. I was so afraid I'd lost him."

"Well, you haven't, and you have lots of fun times ahead in this beautiful spot."

Her mother wiped her tears and smiled. "It's a bit much, I know, but we had lots of fun buying it, fixing it up, and making it our own."

"Better get going. Commercial flights wait for no one, unlike private jets," Bella said, giving her mother one last hug.

As the plane took off, Bella found herself crying, already missing her parents, but they were also tears of joy. She was returning home, returning to the love of *her* life.

CHAPTER 29

Tom met her in the late afternoon. She'd taken a rare direct flight from Naples to Phoenix where Spark's helicopter awaited. Micky had landed the helo in the open fields of Spark's estate. After they thanked him profusely, declining an invitation to dinner, they were on their way.

"Wondering why your boyfriend didn't come?" he said as he pulled out of the long drive.

"No, he texted last night saying he was going to Sonoita with Harley. To pick up horses?"

"Three new mustangs fresh off the meat truck. Ben Morgan heard about them from a friend. One of them's a Morgan, and he's a sucker for Morgans."

"A wild Morgan? That's unusual, isn't it?" she said, gazing over at him.

"Abandoned Morgan. He apparently hooked up with two wildies, and they were rounded up together. They were headed for Mexico and the dog food factory before Ben intervened."

"Poor things," Bella said. "Think how many others never catch Ben Morgan's attention."

"Whip and Harley'll be back midday tomorrow. So, tell me about Mom and Dad."

She spent the ride home filling him in, even though they'd talked nightly while she was in Florida. "I'm trying to get them to come out, but you know they'll at least be coming for the wedding. When are you and Grace going to set a date anyway?"

"Soon."

"That's as specific as you can be, soon?"

"Grace's trying to figure out what to do about Wilbur and his drinking. She's afraid to leave him alone. I've told her he can live out here, but she knows he'll refuse, and, honestly, I don't think she would want that. They've talked about maybe having Gracie move in," he said, referring to the diner owner, Wilbur McGraw's younger sister.

"Poor Gracie."

As they pulled up and Tom shut off the truck, Bella sighed. "It's so good to be home."

"Glad to hear you say home. We missed you."

"Me too, you," she said, smiling over at him.

WHEN NOT WITH THE MUSTANGS, Whip spent the entire time in Sonoita planning what he would say and do when he saw Bella. So much had happened in the past two weeks, and there was so much to tell her. When Harley went into the office at Sonoita Rodeo, the stables where the horses were currently housed, Whip pulled out his phone and called her.

"Hey," he said softly when he heard her voice. "Where are you?"

"Hi. We just got back. Where are you?"

"Sonoita. Waiting for Harley. Local guys are putting us up, and we'll start home first thing with the horses."

"I'm looking forward to seeing you," she said, her voice shy and tentative.

"Can't wait. That's why I'm calling. Are you free later tomorrow, after four or so?"

"I'm putting in a half day at work, but I should be free by then. What did you have in mind?"

"Trail ride?"

"Is it safe."

"No cougar sightings for the past two weeks. We'll stay pretty local. Follow the river, stay out of the hills."

"Sounds great."

"I'll grab something for us to eat, and we can stop somewhere."

"I could always grab something in town on my way home?"

"Thanks, but I've got this. See you tomorrow at the barn around four thirty?"

"Perfect."

They rang off, and Bella carried her laundry downstairs, a wide grin on her face. Tom spied her going by on her way to the laundry room. "What's that shiteater about?"

Bella curtsied. "Wouldn't you like to know."

CHAPTER 30

After a hectic return to work, Bella hurried home and showered, throwing on jeans and a slightly nicer top than she'd normally choose for a trail ride. The beaded vee-neck showed off the curve of her breasts, and the mauve color brought out the softness in her eyes. On the way out, she left a note for her brother and grabbed her backpack and faded denim jacket from the hook by the back door.

When she walked into the barn, the guys called hello as they went about the task of bringing the horses in for feeding and brushing. "Hey, Bella," Greg said. "He's up in the far paddock. Says would you meet him there. The horses are all set."

Bella thanked him, wondering why Greg's eyes seemed to be holding some kind of secret. "Everything okay?"

"Far as I know. Have fun," he said, unsuccessful in hiding a smile as he turned to feed Dusty.

Hmm... Now what? she mused, climbing the rise. As she neared the paddock, she saw Whip, elbow on the fence, chatting with two of the men. She loved the easy way he carried himself, his lean strength, his smile, and the way he interacted with his colleagues. There was a reason why they listened to him, strove to be like him, and respected him completely. In jeans and a faded blue Valley Stables T-shirt, he was the quintessential cowboy, like Harley and few others.

When Whip spied her, he ended his conversation and headed down, tipping his hat as they neared each other. "Am I glad to see you." He opened his arms.

"You too," she said, hugging him tightly, wishing she never had to let go. She felt her body heat rise and knew if he'd invited her to drop her jeans and straddle him right there, she wouldn't have hesitated, damn the audience.

He kissed her hungrily, then stepped away. "You still up for a ride?"

"I am," she said as she noticed the saddled horses in the pen behind them. "That isn't...? Is it?"

He grinned from ear to ear, his gray eyes sparkling. "Yup."

"In two weeks?"

"Yup."

"But how? I can't believe it. It's almost a miracle. Is it even safe?"

"That's a lot of questions, babe. Short answer—the combination of treatment on his mouth and being back with his herd has made all the difference. And, yes, he's safe. I've taken him on three rides this week and he behaved perfectly. He loves it on the trail. You're on Swallow. She's his favorite. Greg and I took them out this morning and had a great ride."

"If you say so."

"If you're nervous with a wildie, I can put you on Calico," he said, referring to his Appaloosa. "I haven't tested them together, though."

"Swallow is fine," Bella said. "She's a calm, beautiful girl. It's amazing how she's filled out in a such short time."

As they headed to the paddock gate, Whip nodded. "Thank Grace for how she looks. When she's through working with Dusty, she's been brushing Swallow and Star, giving them extra treats, you name it."

As they approached the horses, Bella found her heart beating faster. Ghost eyed her briefly, but most of his attention was on Swallow and Whip. "I brought a couple of waters," she said, opening her backpack. "Do you have room for them in the saddlebags."

"Sure do," he said, stowing them. "You can leave the pack, unless you need anything that's in it?"

"Just my pepper spray," she said, pulling the bottle out.

"There's a small pocket at the back of your saddle. Stick it in there. I have some too and the shotgun."

After Bella stowed the can of pepper spray, she stood on Swallow's left side, taking hold of the mare's lead and the saddle pommel. She leaned back slightly, placed her foot in the stirrup, and easily pulled herself up to sit. Swallow took of few steps forward, but was settled and calm. As Whip helped her get the other foot in the stirrup, he said, "Guess Greg was right. You didn't need the steps."

"Now for you," she said, clicking as she turned Swallow. The mare walked to the opposite side of the corral. As Bella watched, he mounted the stallion in a fluid, easy motion. "I still can't believe it."

Whip whistled to one of the men to open the gate, and off they went. "I thought we'd stick to the Loop Trail, then branch off and follow the river a ways," he said. "There's more shade, and we can find a place to stop and water them. Ghost loves it along the river."

"Lead the way!" she said, patting Swallow's withers. "Good girl, let's go."

As they followed the huge white stallion, she marveled at Whip's control and felt sure a weaker rider would not have been able to handle the horse. *Certainly not me*, she mused, *but then those two are bonded.*

Ghost occasionally peeked back to check on Swallow, but otherwise trotted comfortably as they started down the Loop. When the path widened, Whip would pause and let the horses come side by side. Then he'd reach out for Bella's hand. At first, this terrified her and she held Swallow's pommel, mane, and reins in a death grip, but as they proceeded, she relaxed. The horses clearly liked to be near one another, and she loved her connection to Whip.

"Pretty cool, huh?" he asked, echoing her thoughts.

"Not just cool, a miracle. I'm surprised my brother sanctioned this."

"He didn't. He thinks I'm riding Calico."

"Oh jeez, more lecturing."

"Come on," he said as they entered an open area with fields on both sides of the trail. He nudged Ghost, and the stallion took off at full gallop, Swallow following. The mare couldn't keep up with the strong beast ahead, but she moved gracefully and surely, with Bella breathless in the saddle.

As they neared the end of the open space, she called, "Thanks for the warning."

"Never would have let him go except I knew you're as experienced in the saddle as I am."

"Hardly," she said, laughing.

"There's a cutoff ahead that leads to the river, okay?"

"You're the boss."

They rode along the water for several miles, the languid Gila to their right. As they reached a clearing with a grassy setback, he called, "This is a good place to stop."

They dismounted and brought the horses down to the water. Had Whip been on Calico, he would have let him go, but instead, he stretched out the reins so both horses could reach the water, then tied them to nearby trees. Bella watched him take care of the animals, his eyes continually scanning their surroundings. "This place is almost like a staging post," she said as he joined her in the shade.

"Now all it needs is a comfortable bench, but a horse blanket will have to do," he said, moving to unpack the saddle bags. He took out the water bottles, sandwiches, and cheese and crackers, and finally a bottle of Saguaro Pinot Noir and two plastic glasses. "Would have brought champagne," he said, setting everything on the blanket, "but keeping it cold was a problem."

Bella smiled. "And no one likes warm champagne. Are we celebrating?"

He gave her a shy smile. "Truth is I don't much like champagne or most wines. I'm a cowboy. What can I say?"

"You didn't answer my celebrating question."

"You coming home, of course, and Ghost's progress. Swallow's too." He uncorked and poured the wine, then handed her a glass. "How are you? Tell me all about the trip."

"Not much to tell. Dad's fine, just has to take it easy. My parents have morphed from ranchers into Florida nouveau riche. Their house is ridiculously large for two people, they have a bunch of hired help, and they've taken up golf and all kinds of Florida activities, including pickle ball and water aerobics. A personal trainer comes to the house every day to put them through their paces too. It was good to see them, though, so I'm glad I went. You'll meet them sometime whenever my brother and Grace tie the knot, maybe sooner. Now, enough about me. Tell me about the past two weeks!"

He told her about the training and breakthroughs with Ghost as well as his progress with Haley. Observing him, Bella realized she'd never seen him so calm and relaxed. As he finished talking, she remarked on this difference.

"Haley, Ghost, and all this," he said, waving a hand back and forth between them. "It's all helped me recognize what I really want, what's possible, and what I can't live without. That's a first for me as I'm used to pushing through each day, never stopping, never thinking till I hit the bed at night. I've been living like that for over thirty years."

"I'm glad," she said, leaning forward to kiss him softly. "So, what do you want? What's possible and what can't you live without?"

"All the answers come back to you," he said. "I think, but am not one hundred percent sure, that it's possible for me to be close to you and the others in my life who I've pushed away for years. I think you know that I want you more than I've ever wanted anyone or anything. Ever. I also know that there's a lot of things I can live without, but the one thing I can't is you."

He turned away and grabbed something behind him. As he faced her again, his fist was wrapped around a small blue velvet box. "Since I couldn't travel all the way to Florida, I had a talk with Tom the other night."

"Oh?" she said, eyes wide.

"And he gave me permission to do this."

"Do what?" she asked, her eyes sparkling with tears.

"I love you, Bella, beyond all reason. There are tons of things I can live without in this world, but I know with certainty that I can't live another day without you. I know I'm just a cowboy, so beneath you in so many ways."

"Yes," she said, answering the question he had not yet asked.

Whip continued as if he hadn't heard. "I'm not nearly good enough for you, but I can do better, much better. I will work every day to be better for you."

"Yes," she whispered, nodding.

"I'm going to ask you something, and I don't expect you to say yes right away, especially since you seem to be agreeing about the 'not good enough,' 'beneath you' stuff, but if I don't ask, I'll regret it for the rest of my life. Bella, will you make me the happiest cowboy in the world and marry me?"

As he opened the tiny box to reveal an exquisite ring, one lone diamond ringed by tiny sapphires, she leapt forward, throwing herself into his arms. "Yes, yes, yes, I'll marry you! I've been trying to say yes for the last five minutes. I love you more than words can express! You are not beneath me in any way shape or form, Whip Kittredge. You are the most incredible man I've ever met, and I love you so much. I cannot imagine living another second without you!" She showered kisses on his forehead and cheeks, finding his lips at last.

Breathless with longing, he broke the kiss and gazed down at her. "You said yes."

"Of course, I did!"

"So, now can I give you this?" He took the ring from its place.

"It's beautiful," she said, holding out her hand as he slipped it on. "Perfect fit."

"It was my grandmother's. Johnny was supposed to have it, for the woman he married. My mom shipped it to me last week."

"I love it, and I love you," she said, straddling him, hips moving over his arousal.

Whip grinned. "You know, this is a pretty public trail. Anyone could come along..."

"Do you care?"

"Did you really say yes?"

"I certainly did," she said, moving off him to slip out of her boots, jeans, and panties.

"Well, I suppose I should be worried about my future wife's reputation," he said, already unzipping his jeans and releasing his cock.

"Well, I'm not, fiancé," she whispered in his ear as she stroked him.

Whip leaned back and pulled her on top of him, slipping into her hot, wet depths. "Home," he sighed.

Bella moved over him, head thrown back, lost in blinding sensation as he cupped her breasts and gave himself to her.

As they collapsed, drenched in sweat after an explosive climax, they heard voices coming from north of them. Laughing, they dressed quickly, and were almost put together when Nick Parker and a stranger came into view.

"Whoa," Parker said, gazing around. "I've been on vacation for the past week and just got back. This is my friend, Daniel, from Tucson. Not sure what to be surprised about. You two or Ghost with a saddle on his back."

"Great to meet you, Daniel. We're getting married!" Whip cried, coming forward to shake the man's hand.

"Congratulations," Nick and this stranger, who seemed more than a friend to him, said simultaneously. Nick added. "We're going to keep going and let you celebrate. I want to hear everything about Ghost another time. See you." With that, they cantered down the trail out of sight.

Whip pulled her close, kissing her sweetly. "Have I told you how much I love you?"

Bella smiled, running her fingers through his hair. "Several times, my love."

"I'm sorry if I went public without asking you."

"I couldn't be happier, although we'd better get back and tell Tom, or I'll never hear the end of it." She kissed him again.

"I'm with you babe."

"I'll clean up, and you grab the horses."

A few minutes later, they were riding side by side, hand in hand, along the trail. "Come here," he said, leaning toward her. Miraculously, they managed a brief kiss. "I'm warning you now."

"About what?" she asked, looking ahead to the narrowing trail.

"That I'm planning to love you more every day. Can you handle that?"

"That makes two of us," she said, smiling.

"And around that next bend, we're climbing up into open meadow and I'm going to let Ghost go. You ready for that?"

"I love you," she said, "and don't worry, I'll be ready."

Follow me on BookBub for the latest book news and
read on for sample chapters of book one in the Morgan's Fire spin-off
series *Lucy's Hearth!*

LUCY'S HEARTH

Chapter 1

Lucy came home to an empty house. She had really enjoyed having Gus Casey staying in the apartment over the garage. Now he was gone, back to his job at Valley Stables in Arizona. She thought back to the week in Saguaro Valley with her mother, where she'd met Richard Morgan, the man with whom she had just gone riding.

How do I feel about Richard? The longing in his coal-black eyes as he helped her off her horse. She knew he wanted to kiss her, but she had pulled back. *Why? I'm attracted to him, so why not? He's good-looking, filthy rich, and fun. But love? That was with Rob. Our love was supposed to last forever. Instead, my heart's in a million pieces, and I'm not sure how to pick them up.* Her sister Harriet's recommendation was to see Elise, her therapist. *What could be easier?*

She and Rob had met in college when he was a struggling pre-med student. They married during his residency. Rob's parents, now deceased, had built the home Lucy shared with her two teenagers. It was left to Rob and his older sister, Corky, along with another house on Cape Cod. Upon the parents' death, Corky had insisted on having the Cape Cod house, which she promptly sold for an enormous sum. Then, proceeds in hand, she moved to California to become an actress. Last they heard she was out of money and no closer to an acting career than when she had left New England.

Rob and Lucy lovingly restored every inch of the rambling Dutch colonial. Its exquisite woodwork and fine details gave it the appearance of an antique home. Most of the furniture—excepting the most valuable pieces, which Corky had also insisted upon having—had stayed with the house. There were five bedrooms on the second floor. The master suite at one end and then Robert's and Amy's rooms at the other. They kept one room as a guest room and the fifth bedroom had been converted into an office for Lucy's business, a mail-order catalog, Merlin's Closet, specializing in children's books. Now booming, her business had since moved to office space in town.

Lucy looked for a note but found nothing on the kitchen counter except an assortment of dirty dishes, empty milk cartons, and scattered crumbs. She liked a well-ordered house where everything had its place and where one could relax in serenity, not chaos. The first floor of the house had a huge kitchen-family room, a stone hearth at one end, and a recently completed bay window addition at the other. They ate most meals in the light-filled breakfast nook, seated around a burnished maple oval table. On either side of the bay window were two narrow leaded glass panels made by her mother, deep blue morning glories twined round each other reaching toward the sun.

A large family room, smaller wood-paneled den, and solarium were at one end of the house. Off the kitchen was a formal dining room with a fieldstone fireplace, and behind the kitchen, a laundry room, mud room, and bath, as well as a cubbyhole of a room that Rob had used as his home office. A comfortable house, Lucy prided herself on making it even more so in the fifteen years she had lived there.

As she straightened the den, the back door slammed. She paused. "Hi, I'm back here. That you, Rob?" she called, listening for her son's voice.

"It's me, Mom!" her daughter Amy called, popping her head around the den door as her mother scooped up a pile of Sunday papers.

"Hi sweetie, where've you been?" Papers put aside, she hugged her fourteen-year-old.

"At the Robinsons'. They're going out to dinner, so I came home. They asked me to go, but I thought I'd better not 'because I couldn't get you on the phone. How was your ride?"

"Bumpy."

"You've been spending a lot of time with Mr. Morgan, huh?"

"Some. Is that okay with you?"

"Course, what do you think?"

"It's just...with your dad and all."

"Dad has hideous Chloe, so why shouldn't you date?"

"Now, now." Lucy loaded Amy up with an armful of papers and watched her head into the kitchen. Her hair, so like her grandmother's and her Aunt Harriet's, trailed in one thick chestnut braid to her waist. She even walked like Helen, as Lucy herself did. While Lucy favored her father in appearance, with the same pale blue eyes and sandy hair, her gait and mannerisms were her mother's and now, her daughter's as well. Amy most definitely had the Gifford swagger. It suited her.

"Aunt Harriet called," Amy said over her shoulder. "She's stopping by."

"Thanks, sweetie!"

Richard Morgan drove up to his sprawling farmhouse, the first building completed on the property just north of Horseshoe Crab Cove. Fifty-three years old, he had been a widower for nearly two decades. Since his wife's death, he hadn't met anyone like Lucy Winthrop Brennan. She was the first woman since Laura with whom he could imagine sharing his life. He'd dated, so many he'd lost count, but those relationships petered out after a few months.

There is something about Lucy. A wounded bird, yes, but with a depth of soul. He sat on the porch glider and closed his eyes, picturing her soft peach skin, sky-blue eyes, and the way she crinkled her nose when she smiled. He longed to stroke her slender arms, or better yet, drape them over his shoulders and draw her close, but he sensed she wouldn't welcome such gestures. As he let out a deep sigh, a voice called.

"Hey, Dad! You awake?" Weezie, his youngest daughter, bounded up on the porch, followed by her brother Rich, his eldest. Rich was CEO of Morgan Enterprises. He oversaw all his father's businesses, including the new farm. Behind the others came Gail, one of his middle children. Gail and Weezie still lived at home. Gail did publicity and odd jobs for Morgan Enterprises. Richard was constantly encouraging her to spread her wings, but so far, she hadn't wanted to leave the nest.

Richard grinned. "Well, well, well, to what do I owe this pleasure? Are you triple teaming me this morning?"

"Something like that," Rich said, pushing a lock of long sandy hair from his forehead as he set down a bulging briefcase. "Don't you remember? We're having a business meeting." Rich was Laura's child. Same smile, same sandy hair, Laura's soft hazel eyes. He also had her quiet, steady temperament, which made him so effective in his job as CEO.

"Dad's head is in the clouds, daydreaming about his new girl-friend," Weezie said in a singsong voice.

Gail rolled her eyes. "Don't be ridiculous."

Weezie stuck out her tongue at her sister.

Richard threw his hands up. "Okay, okay, girls. No squabbling. Come on inside."

He put his arm around Gail, whom he called his little hedgehog. She'd always been his prickly child. Ninety percent of the time, Gail's brow was wrinkled with a frown. He wished he could change that, but for twenty-six years, he'd been largely unsuccessful. Weezie pushed by, swinging open the door with a flourish, receiving another eye roll from her sister. A study in contrasts, the sisters. Weezie, petite and slender, her dark brown hair cut short in a stylish pixie, choco-late eyes dancing with light. Gail, short too, but all curves, with hazel eyes, her shoulder-length auburn hair held back by a slim leather headband, and freckles splayed across her nose. They both had cute turned-up noses, but the resemblance ended there. Audrey Hepburn and Rita Hayworth, Richard sometimes called them.

Once the four were seated at the dining room table with coffee or water, Richard said, "You're the boss, Rich. Why don't you get us started?"

Rich pulled several folders from his briefcase. "Thanks, Dad. So... construction is pretty much on schedule for this first phase. Barns are looking great. Gus ordered most of the equipment and tack before he left."

"Gee, I wish we could've persuaded him to stay longer," Richard said. "But my brother and his partner would have sued the pants off me, I'm afraid. He was perfect for the job."

"Which we're having trouble filling," Rich said.

Weezie looked at Richard. "I can run the mustang program."

"You're a terrific rider, baby," he said. "But the job takes skills you don't have. Not yet at least."

His youngest huffed. "Do too."

"Besides, you've got school."

"I'm taking a leave." Weezie was enrolled in a master's program for social work, but so far, her participation had been minimal.

"Can we please move on?" Gail said.

"Not until I've said my piece," Weezie said.

Rich sat calmly, shuffling through a file. "Dad, I'll defer to you on this. Are we going to discuss who's running the mustang rescue now?"

"No, except to hear if you've got any good candidates." Weezie opened her mouth, and he raised a hand. "Have you?"

"Couple of guys are interviewing tomorrow. Gail and I can handle it. Weezie's welcome to come, and I may ask Dennis to step in since he's the one who worked most closely with Gus."

"Not true," Weezie said. "I spent every day with Gus and the horses."

Smiling at his youngest, Richard said, "Let's talk about where we are with the thoroughbreds."

"Scouts are looking. It's not easy. Uncle Ben and his buddy grabbed up some of the best this past year for Valley Stables."

"Gail, where are we with branding? We've gotta come up with a name for this enterprise before long, or no one's gonna pay us a bit of attention."

"We're working on it, Dad, I promise. Morgan's Run East isn't gonna cut it, though."

"Agreed," her father said. "What about the wild horses? Where are we with them?"

"Gus thought we should start with no more than five mustangs, but there's such a pressing need for rescue."

"Think we could push that to ten?" Richard asked.

"Not without a competent experienced trainer," Rich said.

"Maybe I can get Gus to come back for a month or so this winter."

Weezie shook her head. "Not a chance, Dad. He's moved into his beautiful new house, kids are happy, and he's getting married soon."

They talked awhile longer, then Weezie and Rich departed. Gail stayed behind to discuss publicity. Finally, she stood. "I'm going into the Cove. You need anything?"

"Thanks, sweetie, I'm fine. I may persuade Lucy to have dinner with me later, but Callie can fix you girls something."

Gail frowned at the mention of Lucy Brennan. "Mom would have loved it here."

He patted her hand. "Maybe. She sure loved Maine after all our years as vagabonds." As he watched Gail gather her things, he thought, *If I get serious with Lucy, my little hedgehog is going to pull out all the stops to break it up.*

Chapter 2

Lucy's partner, Lolly LaSalle, was surrounded by a wall of boxes when Lucy arrived at the office, lunches from the Cove Grille in hand. "I see you've been consorting with the enemy," Lolly said, noticing the bags. Her ex-in-laws, Rosa, and Cesar Rodriguez, owned the Grille. Lolly remained friendly with the couple and several of their offspring, but rarely patronized their very popular restaurant for fear of running into her ex. Sandy Rodriguez, her former husband, lived in town and ran a music venue, Sandy's, on the coast north of the village.

"Only way you'll get your favorite sandwich," Lucy said, plunking a bag in front of her.

Lolly rubbed her hands together. "Thank you, thank you! I have dreams about the California burger."

Lucy grabbed two iced teas out of the office fridge and came to join her. "You might need to get a life, then."

"Says you."

"Touché." Lucy smiled, gazing around at their surroundings. "We really need an assistant. We can afford it. We could go after someone who loves books or just hire some muscle for all this. A few hours a week would really help with this mess."

"If it's muscle you want, we could put a notice up in Averill's," Lolly said, referring to the village's general store.

"Or I could ask Rob if any of his friends would be interested. He's been working after school for his father, so I can't ask him to do this too."

"We could beg him to quit that job and come here."

"No, thanks. Last thing I want is for him to be in the middle of a turf war."

Lucy's ex-husband, Rob, was an internist and ran a family medical practice in the village. He had two associates, and between them, several nurse practitioners and three nurses, they served a number of towns north and south of the village. They maintained their office here because it was central and cheaper. Lucy spent part of every day wishing Rob would move somewhere else, preferably Timbuktu.

"What's new with the unmentionable anyway?" Lolly asked.

"Nothing I want to know about."

"What about the creepy girlfriend."

Lucy put up her hand. "Stop! New subject."

Lolly gave her a mischievous look. "Okay, so what's up with Mr. Hunky Farmer?"

"Nothing. We're friends."

"Does he know that?"

"No, but I'm going tell him tonight. I'm just not ready for more."

"Is it because your ex is still lurking around?"

"No." Lucy threw her sandwich wrapper into the trash. "Let's talk about the mess that's surrounding us, okay?"

"You mean your idiot doctor and my sleazy music promoter?"

"Enough! I'm going to start unpacking these. We've got orders up the wazoo, and some of them need to go out today."

Hands on hips, Lolly stood beside her. "Fine, fine, grouchy, but I want to hear all about your hot date tonight."

"I'm not listening!"

"You look nice, Mom," Amy said as Lucy came downstairs to wait for Richard. "Is Mr. Morgan picking you up?"

"Yes, in about ten minutes. You gonna be okay till Rob gets home?"

Her daughter rolled her eyes. "Mom!"

"Sorry. I'm surprised you didn't join your brother and Dad for dinner. They went to the Clam Shack, I think."

"I have a ton of homework."

"But you have to eat."

"And I did. The leftover lasagna and salad were perfect."

"Okay, I was just wondering, 'cause you love the Clam Shack."

"Yeah, but I hate Chloe, and I didn't want to sit through another dinner listening to what a great massage therapist she is. Yuck!"

Lucy smiled, ruffling her daughter's hair. "You don't have to hate Chloe for my sake."

"Don't worry. She's detestable enough on her own, believe me. She's a complete bitch. I don't know what Dad sees in her."

Youth, Lucy mused. *Youth, energy, new and exciting.* "Well, sweetie, I see Richard's car. I'll be back early."

"Don't hurry home on my account!" Amy called as she closed the front door.

"Wow, you look spectacular!" Richard said as she strolled down the front walk.

Lucy smiled. She'd taken great care with her casual outfit, choosing a top and slacks that flattered her slim figure and silver and lapis jewelry that brought out the blue in her eyes.

"Thanks, so do you."

And he did in slacks and a dark-green linen sports shirt. Like his brother Ben, Richard looked fifteen years younger than he was, with craggy chiseled features, a strong jawline, and those eyebrows, dark like his eyes. He kissed her lightly on the cheek, then escorted her to the car, one hand on the small of her back. His touch was light but firm. After a year of raw nerves, sadness, and grief, his touch was comforting. Lucy felt safe for the first time in many months.

Richard peered around the Cove Grille. The décor was a mix of nautical and Hispanic, but somehow it worked. They were seated by the window overlooking the harbor. "So, this is my first time here. What's good?"

"Everything. Cesar and Rosa are amazing cooks. I always get seafood, but people love the pasta dishes and the enchiladas and all. You really can't go wrong."

"It's a pretty eclectic menu, isn't it?"

"Changes every month."

"Hi, guys, I'm Carla." A pretty twenty-something dressed in denim capris and a gingham top greeted them, pad in hand. Pencil stuck in her ponytail, she pulled it out, unleashing a strand of auburn curls. "Can I start you with a drink?"

"You're new," Lucy said, smiling at her.

"Yup, just started this week. Love it." She bent down and whispered, "My boyfriend Sandy's parents own it."

Richard suggested they get a bottle of wine, and after Lucy's approval, Carla disappeared.

"Oh gee," she said. *Poor Lolly!*

"Second thoughts about the wine?" he asked, concern in his gaze.

"No, the wine's perfect. Our perky waitress is apparently dating my partner's ex. Kind of an ongoing nightmare."

He smiled. "Perky's a perfect description. I would imagine it's rough in a small town after a divorce."

She nodded. "Yes."

"Still difficult for you? I hear that your former husband is the town doc."

"One of them. I have my moments," she answered truthfully. "But it is what it is. If you'd asked me a year ago, I'd have given you a different answer, and if you ask me three years from now, there'll probably be yet another. It's a process, grieving for what's lost forever. People say it takes five years to feel normal again, so I've got a ways to go."

He reached across the table and took her hand. "I'm sorry."

"Thanks. I'm working on it. That's the best I can say. Now let's talk about something more interesting. Tell me about the farm and how things are going. You had just gotten started on our ride."

Carla returned and poured the wine, after which they each ordered the seafood special, pistachio-crusted sea bass, then chatted amiably about their days, his hopes for the farm, and Lucy's business. "We really need to hire an assistant," she said, setting down her fork. "This fish is delicious, isn't it?"

"Yes, it is, and I might know someone."

"Oh?"

"My son Wolfie. Did you meet him at the wedding?"

"Just for a minute," she said, "then I never saw him again."

Richard smiled. "That's Wolfie. He's an introvert. Hermit might be more like it. Weezie's the opposite. I was surprised when he said he wanted to come with us to the wedding, but I think it was an opportunity to see that part of the country."

"Did he have a good time?"

"Stayed at the reception about five minutes, but I think he enjoyed himself. Took lots of hikes. Borrowed a mountain bike a couple of times from Lang Dillon."

"Is he looking for work?"

"Maybe. He loves books. Works in a bookshop in Boston but says he's giving up his apartment and coming home for a while. He likes this area much better than Maine. He's got one year left at Northeastern but has taken the year off. Won't tell me why."

"Well, if he's interested, please have him be in touch. We really do need someone, and a book person would be a huge plus."

Chapter 3

"This really is a beautiful little village," Richard said as they walked out of the restaurant.

She nodded. "It's pretty special. Thank you for dinner."

"My pleasure. I hope we'll have many more. Care for a walk before we head back?"

"We can walk the boardwalk in whichever direction you'd like."

"You choose."

Lucy pointed southwest, where the land curved past the Fishery and Lab, eventually reaching the point and open sea. "Let's see... the streets are quaint and pretty in that direction, but this way is more scenic, more open space."

"I choose scenic," he said. *Although all the scenery I need is standing next to me.*

"Okay." She turned east to follow the boardwalk that skirted the entire west side of the peninsula.

"This is an incredible feat of engineering," he said. "I've never seen anything quite like it."

"And the upkeep is constant. Every time there's a major storm, it gets washed away, only to be rebuilt."

"So, how'd you wind up in Horseshoe Crab Cove anyway?"

"My mom. Well, my parents, actually. They bought a summer place here. Our mother kept it after the divorce. We've spent our summers here since childhood but moved here full-time after the divorce."

"Oh?"

"My father was a train wreck. Still is in some ways."

"Does he live nearby?"

"No, he's in Mattapoisett. Bought a condo with his second wife. They moved there a couple of years ago after he sold the family home in New Bedford."

"So did you grow up in New Bedford?"

"Yes. Those were not happy years."

"I'm sorry."

"I have a dark, checkered past. I hope warning bells are sounding for you."

He paused. They'd reached the edge of the village proper, and open fields stretched to their left. "Quite the contrary."

Before she knew what was happening, he pulled her close and kissed her. His lips were warm and soft as they gently opened hers, his tongue tickling. She responded, arms circled his shoulders, lost in the touch, and feel of him. Her legs grew shaky, and her body tingled with longing. After ten seconds, she shook herself free and stepped back.

He gave her a warm smile, stroking her arm. "Too much?"

"Yes... No... I don't know," she said.

Deer in the headlights, he mused. "It's okay, sweetheart. I'm sure it's obvious that I'm interested in you and have been since we met in Saguaro."

She smiled shyly. "Yes."

"I've dated a lot of women over the past twenty years since my wife died, but never someone like you."

"I'm flattered, Richard. I really am, but I'm just not ready. I had my heart broken by someone I loved very deeply, and I'm still trying to pick up the pieces."

"I can see that, and I won't push you, Lucy, but I'd love for us to be friends."

"Of course." She gave him a mischievous grin. "But friends don't kiss each other like that."

"Maybe not, but you can't blame a guy for trying."

There it was the gorgeous Morgan smile that made women from coast to coast go weak at the knees.

"No," she said softly. "Thanks for understanding. Shall we walk a little farther or turn back?"

"Let's go a few minutes more before heading back. I'd love to see what's ahead."

They passed Lolly's mother's estate, a popular wedding venue with an enormous house, barns, and cottages. Mavis LaSalle was usually booked solid for two years out. Lolly often worked the weddings and sometimes roped her friend in as well. Lucy had served at a number of celebrity weddings over the past ten years. The stars' reps and Mavis herself always had them sign confidentiality agreements before and after such events.

As they headed back to town, he took her hand, and they walked in companionable silence. She felt warm and comforted by his touch. Despite the warning bells, she was very attracted to the handsome fifty-three-year-old. *And Richard Morgan is hot!*

Get Lucy's Hearth today!

ALSO BY M. LEE PRESCOTT

Contemporary Romance

Book 4: *Rich's Dilemma*
Book 5: *Lolly's Wish*
Book 6: *Greta's Goat*
Book 7: *A Horseshoe Crab Cove Christmas*

Well-Loved Romances
Widow's Island
Hestor's Way

Mystery
The Ricky Steele Mysteries
Book 1: *Prepped to Kill*
Book 2: *Gadfly*
Book 3: *Lost in Spindle City*
Book 4: *Poof!*

Also, featuring Ricky Steele:
Jigsaw

Roger and Bess Mysteries
Book 1: *A Friend of Silence*
Book 2: *In the Name of Silence*
Book 3: *The Silence of Memory*
Book 4: *Silencing the Pen*

Young Adult Historical Romance
Song of the Spirit

A NOTE FROM THE AUTHOR

Hope you enjoyed Saguaro Valley's version of Wild Bill Hickok meets the midwife! Like many romances, *Bella's Touch* had plenty of obstacles from her brother's objections to Whip's troubled past, but as you have read, love eventually does conquer all! Grab you copy of *Lucy's Hearth,* the first title in the **Morgan's Fire** spin-off series and travel east with some of your favorite Morgans.

Thank you so much for reading *Bella's Touch* and visiting Saguaro Valley with me. The **Morgan's Run** books are set in the American Southwest, an area of the country that is dear to my heart not only because for many years it was home to my youngest son and family, but also because its beauty is so extraordinary and so startlingly different from that of my New England home. If you enjoyed *Bella's Touch* and are willing to write an Amazon review, I would be so grateful. If you would like to sign up for future book releases, giveaways, and occasional notices about my books, please visit *http://www.mleeprescott.com/* and sign up for my newsletter and follow me on BookBub. I promise I will not share your address, nor will I flood you with emails.

Finally, this book has been revised, proofed, and edited many, many times, but my intrepid assistants and I are human, so if you spot a typo, please email me at *mleeprescott@gmail.com*, and I will fix it.

Warm wishes,

M. Lee

ABOUT THE AUTHOR

M. Lee Prescott is the author of dozens of works of fiction for adults, young adults, and children, among them the Ricky Steele Mysteries, Roger and Bess Mysteries, and a number of stand-alone mysteries and romances. Bella's Touch is number thirteen in her contemporary romance series, *Morgan's Run*. She is thrilled to also have seven books in her spin-off series *Morgan's Fire*, with more coming soon! Three of her nonfiction titles have been published by Heinemann, and she has published numerous articles in the field of literacy education. Lee is professor emeritus at a small New England liberal arts college, where she taught reading and writing pedagogy. Her research continues to focus on mindfulness and connections to reading and writing.

Lee has lived in southern California (loved those Laguna nights!), Chapel Hill, North Carolina, and various spots in Massachusetts and Rhode Island. Currently, she resides in Massachusetts on a beautiful river, where she canoes, swims, and watches an incredible variety of wildlife pass by. She is the mother of two grown sons and spends lots of time with them, their beautiful wives, and her beloved grandchildren. When not teaching or writing, Lee's passions revolve around family, yoga, swimming, sharing mindfulness with children and adults, and walking.

Lee loves to hear from readers. Email her at *mleep-*

rescott@gmail.com, and visit her website to hear the latest and sign up for her newsletters!

Visit my author website and sign up for my newsletter at *http://www.mleeprescott.com.*
Follow me on BookBub *https://www.bookbub.com/search/authors? search=M.+Lee+Prescott*!
If you have five minutes, please review this book!

Made in United States
North Haven, CT
08 November 2022

26446707R00100